IMAGES
FROM
THE
BIBLE

Moses Receives the Law on Sinai
12" x 18", 1960, tempera on paper, collection of Daniel Doron.

IMAGES FROM THE BIBLE

The Paintings of Shalom of Safed
The Words of Elie Wiesel
Introduction by Daniel Doron

The Overlook Press
Woodstock, New York

First published in the United States in 1980
by The Overlook Press, Lewis Hollow Road,
Woodstock, New York 12498
Text Copyright © 1980 by Elirion Associates, Inc.
Paintings Copyright © 1980 by Shalom of Safed
Introduction Copyright © 1980 by Daniel Doron

Bible quotes used with permission.
Copyright © 1917, 1945, 1955 by The Jewish Publications Society of America

Library of Congress Cataloging in Publication Data
Shalom, of Zefat.
    Images from the Bible.
    1. Shalom, of Zefat.   2. Bible. O.T.—
Illustration.   3. Primitivism in art—Israel.
4. Bible stories, English—O.T. I. Wiesel,
Elie, 1928-   II. Title.
ND979.S47A4 1980   759.95694   79-51032
ISBN 0-87951-107-9
ISBN 0-87951-108-7 lim. ed.

Printed in the USA

TABLE OF CONTENTS

Safed—General view of old city.

THE INNOCENT EYE OF A MAN OF GALILEE:

Reflections on Culture, Personality, and Style in Art

Late in the fifteenth century, the town of Safed, high in the hills of Galilee, was a haven for Jews expelled from Spain under the Inquisition. Z'fat, as it is called in Hebrew, became one of the four "holy cities" of Israel, a center of mystical learning, famous throughout the Jewish world for its cabalists, poets, and scholars, and later for its Hebrew press, the first in the Holy land. Today, Safed's mild summer climate draws vacationing Israelis, tourists, and artists, who come there for the spectacular natural setting, and the austere beauty of the old quarter, reminiscent of Granada or Cordoba. Yet of all the painters who have made Safed their home, none has become as famous as a native who lived there for eighty years, familiar to many as "Shalom the Watchmaker."

Shalom's great-grandparents were carried on the wave of messianic longings, that swept the Hassidic movement in the eighteenth century, and brought them from Eastern Europe to Safed. Having lost his *melamed* (teacher) father, Shalom was forced to undertake the support of his family in early adolescence. For more than half a century, he worked at various crafts, all self-taught, mainly as a watchmaker, but also as a scribe, a stonemason, and a silversmith. After the First World War, during which the Turks exiled nearly all the Jewish inhabitants of Safed to Damascus and to Constantinople, Shalom emigrated to Australia, where some relatives had settled in the previous century, after Safed was repeatedly devastated by earthquakes and famine. But he returned home a year later, when he realized that he could not lead a religious life in an alien environment.

Shalom married at an early age, and had a son and two daughters. In the late sixties, he lost his first wife. He later remarried. Until his death in January of 1980, he lived in Safed with his wife, leading a quiet, simple, religious life.

Shalom came to painting late in life. A witty and joyous man, he used to cut out plywood toys for his grandchildren which he decorated with crayons. After the ruin of his watch repair shop in the 1948 War of Independence, he sold these toys through a vendor in Safed's bus station; he barely eked out a living. In the early fifties, a well-known Israeli artist, Yossel Bergner, saw these toys and, recognizing their genuine folk art quality, wanted to meet their creator. The local milkman introduced Shalom to Bergner, who asked Shalom to draw some figures to ascertain whether he was indeed the maker of these toys. When Shalom did, Bergner cried out, "You are like a sackful of good things. Let them out! There will come a time, Shalom, when you will neither eat, nor drink, nor sleep, but paint."

Surprised at the thought, Shalom asked, "What shall I paint?" But he took home a few paints and brushes and soon began setting down the subjects closest to his heart—the events of the Bible as elaborated in Talmudic legends—the Midrashim.

Although he only began painting in the fifties, Shalom of Safed, as he became known, was soon accorded major critical attention on both sides of the Atlantic as a "naif" of outstanding accomplishment. As noted by the French critic Raymond Cogniat, "The mystery of sacred texts that at first seem simple, is reflected in Shalom's poetic compositions, at first glance elementary enough, but proving upon longer study rich in meditative thought and even in profound cultural content." For unconsciously, Shalom recreated a rare art form: giving visual expression to a distinct Jewish sensibility by using the continuous pictorial narrative to illuminate the stories of the Bible.

Continuous pictorial narrative has been employed in the art of many cultures: by the artists who painted on the walls of Egyptian tombs, carved the monumental friezes on Assyrian temples, related the story of Buddha in ancient India, or illustrated Persian miniatures. After assimilating elements of Greco-Roman art, it continued to evolve in Byzantine and Coptic Art and in medieval paintings, tapestries, and illuminations.

Like some of the Jewish artists who adorned ancient synagogues (such as the third century Dura-Europos synagogue) or illuminated medieval Jewish manuscripts (such as the Sarajevo Haggadah), Shalom unconsciously expressed a distinct Jewish sensibility through his own version of the continuous pictorial narrative. Just as the authors of Genesis transformed Hittite and Babylonian myths of creation into a distinct Jewish world-view, some Jewish visual artists, throughout the ages, appear to have adapted narrative art to a unique Jewish style. Consistently avoiding the monumental, the heroic, the perfect and the static styles of ancient and classical art, they used elements from their contemporary art styles to create a life-affirming, dynamic, and intimate artistic idiom.

The way ancient Near Eastern myths were metamorphosed in Genesis reveals the Bible's special outlook. This outlook helped create a distinct Jewish sensibility in some Jewish artists, and particularly in the work of Shalom of Safed.

Early Near Eastern myths depicted creation as the outcome of a violent struggle between contending deities. In the Assyrian creation myth, Marduk, the sun god, fought Tiamat, the goddess of chaos, creating the world out of her vanquished body. Their struggle represented strife between light and darkness, good and evil, order and chaos, male and female. In Greek mythology, too, gods ruling over various aspects of nature battled with each other and with idealized human heroes. In all these myths, the world was created through war, treachery, and bloodshed. Reflecting a dualistic approach to nature, they represented a perpetual struggle between irreconcilable opposites.

By contrast, the Bible stresses the unity of all life and the brotherhood of men created by one God. It depicts creation as a serene and joyous process initiated by God who, as the embodiment of unity, transcends all opposites with His creative will. He creates both light and darkness, separating them out of "the void and the unformed." He names them, gives them both shape and identity, establishes between them both contrast and harmony, as day follows night and the heaven embraces the earth. Like the poet, "as (his) imagination bodies forth, the forms of things unknown . . . (he) turns them to shapes, and gives to airy nothing a local habitation and a name." God takes pleasure in creating. ". . . how good it was," Genesis reiterates after each creative act.

Significantly, God's first creation was light. Light is seeing, understanding. "And wisdom excelleth folly," Ecclesiastes says, "as light excelleth darkness." When we see, we become aware of what is *outside* ourselves, and we achieve self-realization through an awareness of *others*. "The cistern contains," Blake observes, "the fountain overflows." People can be "self-realized" and yet barren, or engaged and fruitful.

In Genesis, God achieves his own "realization," not through self-contemplation, but by creating. Only after actually creating light could He know "how good it was." The mere intent is not enough. God also creates out of ebullience, "overflow," and not merely for self-affirmation. Therefore, His first blessing to His living creatures is "to be fertile and increase." And to man, made in His image, He also gives the gift of creativity.

The God of Genesis differs, then, from the gods of most ancient mythologies. He is not the many-limbed, superhuman monster, triumphing over his enemies, performing heroic feats and miracles. We encounter Him on an intimate, human scale. Upon the peaceful completion of His task, He reviews His work and takes pleasure in it. He contentedly rests on the Sabbath. He is even heard "moving about in the garden at the breezy time of day."

The Bible includes many references to destruction and death in the wider context of creation. Destruction is part of a trial and error process that even God's own creation has to go through. A Midrash asserts that before Genesis, God was creating worlds and destroying them.

Destruction is also the consequence of "wrongdoing," which, like error, is a risk implicit in free choice. Freedom to err is perhaps the greatest challenge God presents to men. The freedom of men to choose enables God to relate to someone who is independent and other than Himself. Had God created an absolutely perfect world, there would be no freedom of choice left; everything

Moses Found in the Bulrushes Mural painting, synagogue of Dura-Europos.

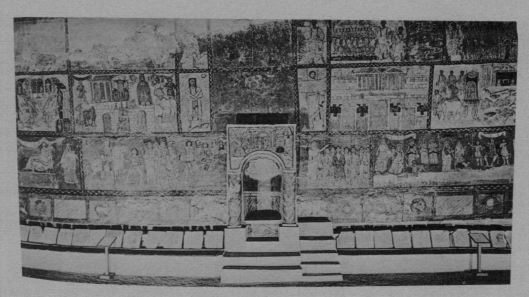

Synagogue of Dura-Europos, Syria   General view of front wall.

would be preordained, and there would be no independent creature to whom God could relate.

For true freedom of choice to exist, not even God may determine the eventual outcome of men's actions. To find out what choice he will make, God put Abraham through a horrible trial, and later allowed the devil to test the virtues of Job, subjecting him to great suffering and even allowing the death of his innocent children (who were never restored to life!). Freedom involves terrible risks. And it is often very costly.

Destruction frequently follows "wrongdoing," but not always. God is prepared to ruin Sodom and Gomorrah, yet Abraham can persuade Him not to "sweep away the innocent along with the guilty." This seems to indicate that creation was necessary not only for God's self-realization, but also for the evolution of justice and mercy through a dialogue between God and those who are independent enough to challenge even Him.

For unlike the gods of antiquity and Greek gods, the God of Genesis is not willful, or capricious in His relations with men. He does not exercise arbitrary power over them, but is bound by justice and mercy. A Midrash insists that the Torah, the law, has preceded even creation, instituting justice and mercy, the dialectical twins enabling men to undergo trial and error and exercise freedom of choice.

To permit freedom to others, God also had to set limits to his own powers. One of these limits was prescribed by mercy, which allowed men to err without incurring the inevitable consequence of destruction. In Greek tragedy, men were captives of inexorable forces, giving them no quarter. Men were instruments of arbitrary and capricious gods, who manipulated their fate, with no regard for justice or mercy. Judaism, however, by affirming men's freedom, implied their responsibility for their deeds.

Fashioned in God's image, men, too, had to set limits to their powers in order to permit freedom to others. Such limits may not enable them to control the world; nor, for that matter, can they always control themselves. Nevertheless, they ought to take responsibility for how they *relate* to others and to themselves. If they err, they should admit their error and repent, just as God repents the destruction He caused in the deluge, and promises never to repeat it.

God, then, accepts responsibility even for destruction. In Genesis, in the midst of the account of the creation of various species it is asserted that "God created the great sea monsters." By this oblique refutation of Babylonian myth—in which the sea monsters were cohorts of Tiamat—it not only denies the divine, independent status of the forces of destruction, but also accepts them as part of God's creation, as His responsibility. Like Caliban, they can not be totally rejected, for they are part of the greater mystery of creation: "The roaring of lions, the howling of wolves, the raging of the stormy sea and the destructive sword are portions of eternity too great for the eye of Man," Blake affirmed.

The Bible's orientation to life and its changes, to justice and to peace — so different from that of all other strife and death obsessed religions of antiquity — reflects a unique world-view. It fashioned a distinct culture and personality type, and affected everything some Jews did, including their artistic expression. A comparison between the works of Shalom and the works of other observant Jewish artists can assist us in identifying elements of a distinct Jewish sensibility in art.

Parenthetically, it should be noted that it makes sense to describe a work of art as Jewish only when the *style* of a work reflects a Jewish sensibility. When a work is only about a Jewish theme, or is merely produced by Jews, it is not necessarily a work of Jewish art. Anyone can paint on Jewish themes in any style, as in fact, many Christian and Moslem artists of all ages did. On the other hand, the works of a Chagall or a Soutine, although produced by Jews, were at least — if not more — reflections of their involvement with the art world of Paris than of their Jewishness.

This is not to imply that a distinct Jewish style in art arises out of a conscious or deliberate decision by an artist to express something "Jewish" in his art. As Shalom's case suggests, style evolves in an unselfconscious and unpremeditated way; the artist need not even be aware of how it expresses his particular heritage. Because creativity is so unselfconscious, an interpreter can sometimes discover in a work of art more than the artist realized was there. Art not only permits but, indeed, encourages the interpreter to read into it more and even different meanings than those intended by the artist. D.H. Lawrence admonished us never to listen to the artist, but to listen carefully to his tale. As long as an interpretation is supported by internal evidence from the work itself, it can deepen our insights into its meaning, and it is a legitimate reading of the work.

Since it is presumed that unschooled artists are incapable of the same degree of profundity and sophistication as trained artists, it is often more difficult to make interpretations of their works credible. Similarly, though on a different level, some critics could not accept the fact that a simple educated actor, William Shakespeare, was the creator of some of the most profound works in the English language.

Yet the profundity of a work of art does not derive from explicit intentions or self-consciousness, though an artist can often intuit the quality of his work without being able to express it in the language of criticism. Of his work, Shalom has said, "It is good when you see and understand and when your hands can do what you see and understand."

A study of Shalom's work should illuminate the relationships among an artist's culture, personality, and style. Because Shalom lived in an isolated community and was unschooled in art, his work was not affected by contemporary visual conventions; it therefore clearly illustrates how his visual style reflected his personality. In addition, such interpretation should shed some light on the nature of art by untrained artists, so-called "naive" art, and how it differs from primitive art, children's art, and the art of the mentally deranged, all of which are often mistakenly lumped together. It should also remind us of how profoundly untrained artists can vary among themselves.

Although representational, the art of Shalom is essentially different in aim, in technique, and in its origins from most forms of Western representational art, including Western naive art. These forms were mainly derived from classical art, which attempted to transcend death and arrest the ravages of time, either by the monumentality of sheer mass and scale, or through idealization—by creating perfect immutable imitations of nature.

In contrast, Judaism accepted and even blessed the passage of time. It was time, and not a place or a person that was the first to be sanctified in Genesis by God, who hallowed the Sabbath, a day, marking the progression of time.

To fashion an iconography to Greek idealism, to its quest for static universals and epiphanies of perfection, classical artists would lift a person or an event out of its context in time, and arrest all change by molding them into immutable and perfect illusions of the "real thing." The heroic, the tragic, were raised on a pedestal and carefully modelled and lighted in dramatized and hieratic poses. Yet however eager these artists were to create the perfect illusion of nature, they were not really interested in particular persons or in actual moments, but in their symbolic, universal significance. Their passion for the figurative was not for a particular figure, but for an ideal, the embodiment of mathematical proportions and golden means, not unlike the passion of romantic sonneteers for their "Stellas." Indeed, like modern non-representational artists, Classical and Renaissance artists were also abstracting from nature. Their abstractions, however, were expressed differently, because they believed that ideal patterns were actually embodied in reality.

Subsequently, the adoration of the ideal was extended from the created image to its creators and elevated post-Renaissance artists to the status of demi-gods, the purveyors of divine Truth. This adulation was further inflated by romanticism and brought to its absurd conclusion in modern times. Given the pervasive definition of personality as the "persona" which separates one man from others, and of originality as radical innovation, it should not be surprising that placing the artist at the center of the universe soon led the artist to look inward. This often resulted in an art of non-communicable private idiosyncracies presented as

The Sacrifice of Isaac by Shalom of Safed,
14" x 22", 1960, tempera on paper,
collection of Daniel Doron.

The Sacrifice of Isaac   Mosaic floor, Beth Alpha synagogue.

some mysterious knowledge that only afficionados and specialized critics could fathom; an art whose significance derived more from interpretation than from its own intrinsic qualities.

The culture which nurtured the art of Shalom had a different conception of reality and of man's place in it. It cultivated a different personality type and fostered a different style of art.

When asked if he did not infringe on the commandment against graven images, Shalom insisted that he "did not paint paintings, but retold the story of the Bible in color and in line." In making this distinction, he shed light not only on a significant formal quality of his art— which was to render an *evolving* reality—but possibly on an important intention of the second commandment. To Shalom, as to other believing Jewish artists, indeed to its Talmudic interpreters, the second commandment did not prohibit all forms of representation. It objected to idealized, sculptural imitations of nature which might attempt to outdo God's work, and which the ignorant, in mistaking for "the real thing," might idolize and worship.

In objecting to the iconography of Greek idealism, Judaism expressed an aversion to all dogma, to the tyranny of abstract, ideal universals. Hebrew, the language of Judaism, is concrete and uncomfortable with abstract formations. Until Maimonides (who wrote much of his philosophy in Arabic) applied Arab Aristotelianism to Judaism and formulated thirteen articles of faith, Judaism was not concerned with doctrines. Its practices evolved as a body of common law, based on rather free, even "poetic" application of sacred writings and principles to daily life. Even the contents of the Scripture were decided upon by human consensus. Faith was a way of living, rather than a concern with the nature of belief. It was only when it donned a self-protective armor of dogma that medieval Judaism—probably in aversion to Christian icon-worship—accepted the interpretation of the second commandment as an injunction against all figurative art. The subtle objection of earlier Judaism to what Whitehead termed "the fallacy of misplaced concreteness," the mistaking of abstractions for living realities, was overshadowed by more urgent concerns.

The acceptance by Jewish tradition of time and change and their concrete, particular expression in the history of the Jews determined the pictorial approach of the artists who—without necessarily being aware of doing so—expressed a distinct Jewish sensibility in the visual arts. Their subject matter was the past history and the future hopes of their people. Their compositions were therefore devoted to the evolution of this story, to the passage of time, to wholeness, rhythm, and action.

In discussing the essence of Jewish art, Dr. Ernest Nemenyi has observed that in the Dura-Europos synagogue murals, which date back to the third century and are the earliest examples

ליד שאון את יונה וישליכו אל הים ויעמד הים מזעפו ויין ה׳ דג גדול לבלע את יונה.

Jonah Being Swallowed by the Fish by Shalom of Safed,
14" x 19", 1963, tempera on paper, collection of Daniel Doron.

extant of Jewish art, "the representation of persons, and the beauty of the human form remain of obviously secondary importance to the artist, who seems not to have been at all concerned with three dimensional representation and . . . the tricks of perspective which he had learned from Greek artists. The general setting of the action . . . its architecture and landscape are his main preoccupation. The element of motion . . . is developed to such an extreme that it distracts our attention from each human figure in turn. We are made to contemplate huge groupings of figures and stretches of time and space in which they move and meet."

Similarly, in a seminal analysis of the sixth century mosaic floor of the Beth Alpha synagogue, depicting the sacrifice of Isaac, Professor Meyer Schapiro discerned "how oblivious the artists seemed to be to the canons of classic style of representation," because of their preference for rendering "an action rather than a fixed state of affairs." Their "sense of pictorial whole" and of "rhythms and correspondences" between individual objects more than compensated for their "innocence of the detailed structure of the human and animal bodies" and for their "loosely ordered" composition, "without an axis or a center."

A stress on motion, rhythm, and wholeness was also the hallmark of Shalom's style. Depicting an *evolving* story required the juxtaposition of a sequence of scenes, a multiaxial composition which, lacking a single focal point, did not permit the employment of formal perspective. Shalom's major formal task was therefore to balance these disparate scenes into a coherent whole. This seems to have come to him easily because he was a visionary artist. "From the beginning," he said, "I see the whole story in front of my eyes, clear as a dream." He put his vision down on the page, letting the action flow in the direction of Hebrew script, from right to left and from top to bottom, except when the action led up to Jerusalem or to the Promised Land, when it ascended the page.

Usually Shalom started painting by making a framework, then outlining the forms, and finally coloring them in an orderly fashion, seldom changing his mind or having to correct himself. But while the whole was prefigured in his mind, details shaped themselves as he worked. As in Mozart's music, a conception of a harmonious whole created a balance between inevitability and surprise, between structure and improvisation. If it seems to have happened effortlessly, it is because his inventiveness was not inhibited by self-conscious considerations of style. His style was himself, and he was the embodiment of a culture that fully integrated its world-view into all its expressions.

Thus, Shalom's compositions accented integration rather than differentiation, giving a sense of coherence and compactness to his work. Since events or people were not idealized, they were not

Jacob Blessing His Sons by Shalom of Safed,
12" x 18", 1960, tempera on paper, private collection.

set apart in splendid isolation nor lifted out of their context in the story. In a work depicting the Exodus, Moses is almost indistinguishable from his followers. In another painting devoted to one of the most momentous events in Jewish history, Moses is seen coming down Mount Sinai surrounded by fire and smoke; because it was a hot day in the desert, Moses—in the painting—was dressed in shorts.

Such irreverent humor was an expression of an anti-heroic tradition in Judaism which can be found in many Hassidic tales and also in Midrashic and Biblical lore. It is evident in the pains the Bible took not to omit or gloss over the transgressions and foibles of even so great a figure as King David (the Bathsheba and the Absalom affairs), and in the fact that throughout the Passover Haggadah, Moses is mentioned but once, apparently in an effort to combat an all too human proclivity for hero worship.

Through its cathartic effect, humor also mitigates some of the horror and pity that tragedy evokes, and helps put it in the context of life's vicissitudes. In a painting depicting the plague of the first-born, Shalom showed all the dead, men and cattle, lying on their backs, except for one lamb, walking away, a curious smile on its face. When asked why, in a painting that depicted Jonah being swallowed by the whale, he added several rows of small fish peeking from the waves, Shalom replied, "It is not every day that they get a chance to see a fish swallow a prophet." In another painting depicting the animals marching in pairs into Noah's ark, Shalom painted only a single elephant. "Noah would have a space problem, so he took only one elephant—a pregnant one," was the explanation he gave.

Everyone, then, was part of the greater creation. People, animals, trees, houses, or clouds were woven into patterns and rhythms that reflected the continuity of time and space in which they met and acted. To convey a feeling of wholeness, Shalom also put at least a trace of the earth and a suggestion of a sky in most of his compositions. However, his world was not only complete, but also purposeful. When asked why he painted a town on the horizon in a painting that should have depicted Jonah being spewed out by the whale, Shalom replied without hesitation, "A man must have a place to go."

The repetition of forms in the various scenes required a high degree of economy and stylization if a crowded world was not to become cluttered, and the coherence of the whole lost in a mass of detail. Shalom delineated his shapes in a visual "shorthand," mostly in profile or silhouette, with no modeling in light and shadow. He adjusted their relative size and proportion to compositional and expressive needs rather than to illusionistic accuracy. Jacob was an important person, so his bed was stretched out.

The separate delineation of forms enhanced clarity. Relations were established by rhythmic groupings and an instinctive sense

The Redeemers Battling at Mount Esau by Shalom of Safed,
13" x 19", 1962, tempera on paper, collection of Daniel Doron.

for the right open spaces. Houses blended into the composition the way towns like Safed used to blend into the hilly Galilean landscape. Stylization, however, never led to standardization, nor was it ever at the expense of the significant detail. Each group of houses was formed to fit its environment. The shapes of animals or birds may not have been anatomically accurate, but how precisely rendered were their stances and movement. Cloud forms expressed a whimsical and inventive imagination, often recalling shapes that Matisse or Picasso might have fashioned.

To Shalom, the events of the Bible did not happen in a distant "chronological" past. To him, Abraham, Isaac and Jacob were as close as his own grandfather, while the prophets' vision of the future was near at hand, too. All towns were Safed. The Philistines were dressed like Turkish foot soldiers from the First World War, while on Egypt's Nile a steamboat chugged along, with a sail added for good measure. Obadiah's prophecy of the redemption of Zion was envisioned as happening during Israel's War of Independence, with a platoon of Haganah fighters firing a mortar at "Mount Esau." However, since in Safed the defenders were poorly armed, Shalom added an airplane to assure victory; his fantasy compensated for the deficiencies of life.

To bring the events of the Bible closer, Shalom telescoped space as well as time. The picture plane was condensed, space was staged and brought forward. Where necessary, depth was achieved by the recession of planes in pure color. Scenes were rendered from different angles. Some were presented from close up in order to draw us into the action, or from afar to give us a wider perspective. Occasionally, objects were spread out on the page so that we could see both sides of an important structure, as when Abraham's house was depicted, or a section was removed so that we could see the people praying inside the synagogue. The freedom to disregard appearances permitted tighter design and greater systematization of areas.

Shalom's love for the concrete, his eye for detail were evident everywhere in his work. When a street lamp was installed in his neighborhood, his paintings blossomed with them. A house of a potentate, or the wall of a fortress city were barred by the door of a safe like that in the bank where his daughter worked; it was a symbol of solidity, prosperity, and might.

Throughout the ages, Jewish interpreters of the Bible considered every verse, phrase, and even letter in the Bible pregnant with significance. Shalom's paintings often referred to such interpretations and their mystical and symbolic allusions. The symbolism was conveyed through the shapes, the colors, or even the number of forms he painted. Trees symbolized life. They often had five limbs spread like the fingers of the cohen (priest), raised in benediction. They also often alluded to the verse in Psalms about the Just man, who shall prosper like "a tree planted on running water," which in an arid land had a decided advantage. In *Night of Redemption* (see p. 106), the role of color in symbolizing meaning was particularly prominent.

Shalom's greatest gift as an artist was perhaps his intuitive understanding of the special light of his land, and how it is transformed into color. Earlier, we discussed the metaphysical significance of the creation of light. For Shalom, light's translucence and opacity expressed indeed the interplay between substance and void, between corporeality and spirit, positive and negative space. Light's warmth or coldness, its reflective and penetrative modes were transmuted into subtle or bold arrays of colors and hues. So attuned was Shalom to the light of Safed that in winter his palette was often rich in neutral tints and subtle shades, while in summer it burst into sharp contrasts and unexpected harmonies and ranges. Some paintings, such as *Receiving the Sabbath* (see p. 85), reflected the dramatic sunsets of Safed. The ethereal pale blues of dusk, the golds, the pinks, and the purples intertwine with the burnt ochres and saturated brown of the earth, infusing, as did the Cabalists, the secular with the holy.

Shalom's handling of paint was very free, and yet it showed a craftsman's discipline and ability to give textural variety to different areas of the composition. Like most artists, Shalom matured, and his innate talents developed with time. Some of his later works, such as *The Exodus* (see p. 110), or *Moses on Sinai* (see p. 108) exhibit a greater subtlety of design, richer color, and a confidence in his skill that enabled him to execute bolder and more complex compositions without losing their basic coherence.

Despite the fact that he knew little or nothing about art, or about historical antecedents, Shalom's work bears curious affinities to some Assyrian, Indian, Coptic, early Byzantine, and Persian art, and to some medieval illuminations, but mostly to the few surviving examples of ancient Jewish sacred art mentioned before.

There are also significant similarities between early works by Shalom and some nineteenth century Palestinian Jewish folk art. There is a particularly strong resemblance between Shalom's two-dimensional toys and works of the most prominent nineteenth century Palestinian artist, Moshe Mizrahi (1870-1930). In Mizrahi's work we find, however, a clear effort to create an illusion of realistic space and to model figures in the round. In contrast to Shalom, who, disregarding perspective, always stood his figures on top of the ground, Mizrahi placed the feet of his figures in the middle of the ground in a further attempt to create an illusion of depth. Mizrahi, a native of Persia, was probably inspired by Islamic folk art common in his birthplace and other parts of the Middle East, a tradition replete with Western influences. Whether Shalom saw Mizrahi's work, a derivative work, or a lost work that inspired Mizrahi and others, like the Hebrew Kashan rug of 1840, which was probably the origin of Mizrahi's work depicting the sacrifice of Isaac, cannot be ascertained. Shalom completely assimilated what inspired him and adapted it to his own style; just as he later adapted images originating in the works of Dürer and Doré, which he saw in a Golden Bible belonging to one of his grandchildren.

Shalom's art represents, then, a unique blend between a literary tradition—the Hassidic heritage and the mystical lore of the Cabala—and the artist's sensitivity to the light and landscape of the Galilee. It is this unique blend of the universal elements of a strictly literary tradition with the visual elements of a particular locality that makes Shalom's art so distinctly Jewish and Israeli.

In its freedom from the strictures of classicism, Shalom's style was close to the idioms of modern art. However, the vision which he expressed in his art was quite different from that of most modern artists. Having never idolized man, Shalom was not smitten by the "existential plight of man." It was a matter of course to him that human life, like that of all animals, was a trial. Therefore, he was neither obsessively preoccupied with fashioning "anxious objects," nor did he narcissistically project human plight on the entire universe. Since he never idealized nature, he was not impelled to outdo its creations, and failing, to retreat into minimalist reductionism. Never having lost his childlike capacity to grasp and express the essential simplicity of things, Shalom did not have to seek innocence in regression, nor directness in automatism.

Above all, Shalom's visual statement was a testament to an existentialism of hope that contrasted with the existentialism born of despair, that since Kierkegaard, seems to have haunted modern man's sensibilities. It affirmed his faith that life did have a meaning beyond our grasp, a meaning which we may always have to struggle to discover, but that consisted not only of ugliness and pain, but also of beauty and joy; that tragedy was also comic, and that, at least in artistic fantasy, discord could be resolved so that people would experience their potential for goodness. If this vision does not appeal to the self-indulgent morbidity of our age, and therefore seems irrelevant, perhaps it is worth recalling that in their last and most mature works, both Shakespeare and Mozart expressed similar hopes. In the romances, as in *The Magic Flute*, discord was resolved and goodness triumphed, not because their creators were oblivious to the human condition, but because they apparently believed that life was greater even than tragedy, and, as their very works attested, creation was more encompassing and perhaps more everlasting than destruction.

Since much of the contemporary interest in naive art is the result of weariness with over-sophistication, we often mistakenly

The Sacrifice of Isaac by Shalom of Safed,
14" x 6½", 1958, plywood & tempera, collection of Mrs. H. Eccles.

Abraham Leading Isaac to Sacrifice by Shalom of Safed,
7½" x 6½", 1958, plywood & tempera, collection of Mrs. H. Eccles.

Eliezer & Ishmael Attending by Shalom of Safed,
14" x 6½", 1958, plywood & tempera, collection of Mrs. H. Eccles.

assume a dichotomy between innocence and experience, between simplicity and skill. Even sensitive observers who extoll simplicity when it is rediscovered by artists like Klee, Miró or Dubuffet, often condescend to untrained artists by referring to them as primitive, meaning childish or elementary. The relationship of the "innocent eye" to the naive and the primitive should therefore be clarified.

A distinction should first be made between the childish and the childlike, between the naive and the innocent. Children lack experience and the capacity to integrate and articulate it. Their expressive skills are limited. Their art has appeal not because of their childishness, their limitation, but because of its freshness and its unconventionality. For some children have not been dulled by the conflicts that force adults to block their perceptions and employ their intellect in warding off painful experiences with callousness and rationalizations.

If painful experience often destroys innocence, it does not always do so. Such was apparently Blake's conviction when he wrote his *Songs of Experience* as a *sequel* to his *Songs of Innocence*. Such was also the testimony left by Shakespeare and Mozart in their later works. Nor can innocence be restored by rejecting experience, and regressing into infantilism. Only the full assimilation of experience, and its transcendence, can revive a capacity for full response. Only by making the unconscious accessible, can creative impulses which originate in a fusion of sensation, emotion, and reason find direct and free expression without too much struggle, pain, and distortion.

Children's art, primitive art, the art of the mentally deranged, so-called naive art, and the art of contemporary artists share the need to express the unconscious. However, each of these art forms expresses a different state of the unconscious, and does so on different levels of expressive integration and excellence.

Children's art is a hit-or-miss affair because most children lack the skills that are acquired through experience, and also suffer the beginning of inhibition. The few children who escape repression, by the grace of circumstances or by strength of talent, still lack the skill and the awareness that help transform inspiration into consistent achievement.

In comparison with the art of "normal" adults, the art of the mentally deranged is less inhibited, because intellectual defenses have collapsed. What is revealed, however, is a sick, strife-torn unconscious that can exercise great appeal, even mesmerize, yet is usually compulsive and narrow in focus. Since it exposes anxieties and rages that many normal people conceal with effort, it fascinates and can even provide a carthartic effect. It lacks, however, the ordering quality of a healthy intellect that enables the mind to tolerate ambiguities, the negative capabilities which

The Sacrifice of Isaac by Shalom of Safed,
18" x 11", 1958, tempera on paper, collection of Israel Museum.

The Sacrifice of Isaac by Moshe Mizrahi,
1913, lithograph, collection of Dr. H. S. Kaufman.

permit an artist not to resolve such ambiguities prematurely, but to wait for their resolution on a more encompassing level of expression. The ability to tolerate ambiguities and not to resolve them prematurely is usually the hallmark of great works of art.

Primitive art—a term that should be confined to the work of artists living in a rural, tribal society, mostly in Africa, Oceania, and South America—ranges somewhere among the childish, the deranged and the innocent. Often it is simply elementary and uninhibited. In societies that institutionalize derangement, art is possessed by dark powers, by magic, and by compulsive ritual repetitions, often a perverse expression of the basic rhythms of life. Some primitive art that appears to the Western eye as elementary or inept, is, in fact, the product of successive generations of sophisticated, highly skilled and rigorously trained artisans who because of the role of art in religious rituals followed strict conventions. Unfortunately, when contact with technologically superior cultures undermined the society and its beliefs and vitiated the conventions which expressed them, these art styles degenerated too. Relying on fairly rigid conventions that discouraged individuality and innovation, primitive and folk art lost their vitality, and degenerated into mere decoration, forms divorced from feeling.

The art of untaught artists—and there have been very few truly innocent eyes—can preserve the child's innocence while incorporating the skill, the sophistication, and the range of feeling that come only with maturity. Its vision can be fresh and personal, because being unschooled, it is not distracted by conventions. Unfortunately, "naive art" has often become another convention; (so much so that the Yugoslav "school" of peasant artists has established its own academy for naive art!)

Even genuine "naives" have been corrupted after they were discovered. However, the most talented, like Rousseau, managed to remain unaffected by the art world, even after discovery, because they started painting when their personalities were already well formed, and they had developed a distinct way of seeing things. Also, since untrained artists usually started painting late in life, they belonged culturally to a past generation, and they could be oblivious of current visual fashions. They often belonged to isolated rural settlements, to subcultures, and their community had a distinctness that set it apart from the rest of society.

This was also true of Shalom: a native of a small town in the remote reaches of the Galilee, he knew nothing at all about Art. He grew up in a fairly hermetic religious community removed from the secular mainstream of Israeli life. Under the Turks and the British, Safed had a mixed population of Arabs and Jews. The Jewish community, comprised of Sephardic and Ashkenazi Jews, mostly religious-orthodox, lived in close contact in their ghetto-like quarter. It therefore developed a fairly distinct subculture; the language was mainly Yiddish (Hebrew was considered too sacred for everyday discourse) but incorporated many Arabic expressions as well as Sephardic folklore and idioms. The isolation of this orthodox community persisted well into the nineteen-sixties, despite the fact that in the fifties Safed already boasted an artists' colony, made up mostly of weekend residents who subsequently tired of its isolation and moved back to the proximity of the art market in Tel Aviv. This isolation has gradually ended with the brisk development of the town and with the advent of many new immigrants and, of course, television.

Because Shalom was untrained and his work showed the typical disregard of naive artists for the conventions of classical representation, it was often classified as "naive" art: But this designation is at best only partially correct. Despite sharing some characteristics with other untrained artists, Shalom's style and vision are as different from those of most other untrained artists, as they are from all other forms of Western art. With very few exceptions (again, Rousseau comes to mind) most untrained artists evoke childhood memories and landscapes, in a nostalgic fashion. Their sentimental and folklorist concerns confine their work to the strictly anecdotal. Shalom's art reflects a rich heritage, a profound faith, and the visual talents necessary to express them. It recalls in its innocence, intensity and directness, the works of the pre-Giotto Italian primitives, and should be more appropriately classified as a form of sacred visionary art, quite common in medieval times, but very rare in a secular age.

Shalom's visual innocence, his ignorance of artistic conventions, permitted him—as it has permitted other untrained artists —to express his personality more directly in his art. However, since Shalom was so well integrated into his community, his personal idiom was also the universal language of his culture.

Earlier, we noted how Shalom blended patterns of houses into his compositions the way the builders of villages like Safed integrated their buildings into the hilly Galilean landscape. It did not occur to these builders that they must express themselves by devising a unique structure, or at least a different facade for their buildings, the way many Western architects do. A humbleness of means, coupled with personal humility and a full integration in the community made them build the simplest structures from available materials, following the contours of the landscape and its interaction with human activities and needs.

So with Shalom, the lack of preoccupation with an artistic persona that is in conflict with its culture permitted him to escape the common dichotomy between innovation and tradition. Such lack of conflict deprived his work of a driving tension, of the need to be different, and of a sense of drama, but it also protected him from alienation and aridity.

Western culture encourages individuality based on what differentiates each person from another, at the expense of cooperation and harmony. The resulting tension between the individual and his community has brought about great discoveries and many benefits, but has also exacted a toll in excessive rates of social change and in alienation. Traditional and religious societies have subdued individuality to social continuity and cohesiveness. This has often resulted in stagnation and in the formation of monolithic and authoritarian institutions. Paradoxically, however, religious societies, based on individual conformity, have created very distinct cultures; while modern society, which stressed individuality, has become more and more homogeneous.

When Shalom integrated the monotonous cubes of housing units that mar the Israeli landscape into distinct patterns and rhythms that blend so well into their environment in his paintings, he demonstrated again how his religious sensibility reconciled individuality with universality. Comprised of standardized elements, each of his clusters of houses had a distinctness of rhythm, shape, and color harmony suited to its particular landscape, thus reconciling variety with coherence.

"I am a serious man," Shalom said, "I do not paint out of my imagination." That is, he did not believe in foisting upon us a private conception of reality. When painting, he was not concerned with projecting his ego, but with transmitting a tradition. Nor did he try to be original by being unique or different. He considered himself an artificer, an instrument through which the story of his people found a "local habitation and a name."

It is remarkable that while not trying to impose his personality through his art, Shalom created a personal idiom that was an expression of a common heritage, bridging in his art the dichotomy between the personal and the universal by establishing between them a harmony that is pleasing to the eye and nourishing to the soul.

Daniel Doron, 1980

The Plague of the Firstborn
17" x 22", 1961, tempera on paper, collection of Daniel Doron.

IMAGES AND LEGENDS FROM THE BIBLE
by Elie Wiesel

In the beginning God created heaven and earth. But even before that, He had created seven things—including the name of the Messiah, the celestial voice calling for repentance and the Torah, written with black fire on white fire.

At first God was uncertain whether a world inhabited and ruled by man should exist at all. He turned to the Torah for advice and the Torah urged him to go ahead with His project; for a king alone is hardly that: he needs others, so that he may stress his powers over them.

Still the Torah had some reservations. What if man should sin and disobey God's commandments? You need not worry, said God. Both repentance and redemption will have preceded creation.

So would justice and mercy. For while God's first impulse had been to let the world be ruled by justice alone, he later understood that this would not be possible; man would be doomed by his first mistake. So God paired justice with compassion. The combination of the two made creation possible. And worthwhile.

Does that mean that God may have created this world only to let it be destroyed? Yes. This should come as no surprise. It happened before. Ours is not the first world. Others existed before and were destroyed by God because He was not pleased with them. Ours alone pleased him enough to be allowed to remain.

It took Him six days to complete His work.

On the first day he created more than one heaven and more than one earth—seven of each—but only one was visible to man. He thus willed man to become conscious of his shortcomings. Beneath and beyond what his eyes perceive, there are secret palaces which only the chosen can penetrate. Beyond and beneath his kingdom, there are others. The secret of creation lies in creation itself and all that man can do is learn of its existence. Such knowledge is a curse to fools and a blessing to the wise.

On the second day God created a firmament which divided the waters into upper waters and lower waters. This was not done without problems. At first the lower waters refused to obey the order to recede. Only when they heard that God in His anger was ready to change his mind and restore the universe to its primary chaos, did they yield. As a reward, they could praise God at will—while the upper waters required the permission of the lower waters to sing before Him.

Because of this division, God did not say of the second day that He liked what he saw—as He did of all the other days. And it is not surprising that hell was created on that day. Hell is a result of division; hell is division.

On the third day God created dry land, plants and trees. And they all praised His glory and bore witness to His greatness. Endowed with a life of their own, these living things speak to each other and also to mankind, giving joy and enrichment to all those who listen.

Every sprig of grass has its own destiny to guide and protect it. Not one grows without the express order of its angel up above.

Plants and trees are not jealous of one another; they reflect understanding and harmony. So it is not surprising that they fill Paradise, which means that this particularly luminous day also witnessed the creation of Paradise.

But there were also problems with the trees—particularly with the tall and proud cedars of Lebanon. Somehow they seemed to stand too erect, exuding a kind of vanity. So God immediately created iron. The trees understood the menace and began weeping: "Woe onto us.... We shall all be cut down by axes made of iron...." But God reassured them; "Without handles, iron will not turn into axes; since the handles will be made of wood, you must simply prevent your own trees from betraying you; remain faithful to one another and the iron will be powerless against you."

There was so much compassion and friendship in that message, that it was only normal that on that day God looked at His work twice and was pleased.

On the fourth day God created two great lights—one for

the days, another, smaller than the first but still great, for the nights to come. One was the sun and the other the moon.

Naturally, the moon was dissatisfied, and for good reason. It was the moon who had drawn God's attention to the absurdity of having two lights of equal intensity: "Is it possible, Master of the Universe, for two kings to wear the same crown?" God answered: "Go and lower your light." To which the moon replied: "You are punishing me for having said something that makes sense." But God chose not to alter His plan. Still, in order to console and offer some compensation, He told the moon: "Since you have consented to reign over nights, I shall order the stars to accompany you in the evening when you arrive, and at dawn when you leave; at all times shall you be followed by a brilliant procession of lights." The stars were thus created on that very day.

There is another version:

As the moon's lights diminished, it felt such pain and such shame that it fell and, in that fall, innumerable fragments tore from its body. These fragments are still visible; they are the stars. They belong to the moon, not to the sun. And that is why they appear only at night.

On the fifth day God created the birds and the fish and ordered them to multiply in the wind and the water and the swamps. Every species was represented and each had its clearly defined role and place.

Rabbi Akiba saw the greatness of God in this: "There are creatures that grow in the sea and others that grow on earth. Were the first to try land, they would die instantly; were the latter to try the sea, they would die on the spot. Furthermore, there are creatures who feed on fire and others who feed on air; the element proper to the one is death to the other, Their creator has arranged everything so that everything that lives will continue to live and propagate."

Nothing then is useless. Not even the flies, bedbugs and mosquitoes: They are part of creation—God's instruments and also His messengers.

But on that day, God not only created the species but also their masters.

The king of the fish is Leviathan who is monstrous in size. When he is thirsty, he drinks all the water that flows from the Jordan into the sea; when he is hot, he makes the very sea boil.

The king of the birds is Ziz whose wings darken the sun. When he stands in the sea, at its deepest spot, the waters do not reach higher than his ankles—while his head touches the sky.

Both are destined to serve as food for the Just men at the end of time. For they too—as everyone and everything else—live in the continuous expectation of the Messiah.

On the morning of the sixth day God created the cattle and beasts and all the creatures living on dry land. And the sight of them pleased Him, for they were all kind and generous towards one another. Cats and mice lived in peace, as did dogs and cats. The serpent could walk and talk and meant harm to nobody. Things changed only after man had entered their world. Cursed, the serpent began to creep. The first cat quarreled with the first dog—about food—and their hate animates their descendants to this day. The same is true of the first cat and the first mouse. They were created as equals and associates; they shared their food. Then the mouse became hungry and began to complain, so much so that it was condemned to be devoured by the cat. The mouse became so frightened that, to this day, its fear is felt by its descendants.

All of this is meant to teach us that everything happening now is the result of things that happened long ago.

In the afternoon of that day God informed the angels of His decision to create man and make him in His image. Some were pleased, others voiced resentment. The Angel of Love saw man as a vehicle of love and therefore wanted him to come into being—but the Angel of Truth foresaw the lies man would carry and spread, and therefore opposed his being born. The same split occurred between the Angel of Justice and the Angel of Peace. The first was sure of man's ability and desire to practice justice—but the latter was equally sure of man's inability to live peacefully for any length of time. God succeeded somehow in pacifying the Angel of Peace but had to expel the Angel of Truth from heaven before realizing His project. So the Angel of Truth was sent down to earth, there to await man and share his fate—forever.

There were other angels who opposed man and they were all destroyed by fire. Only their leaders—Michael and Gabriel—were saved. So grateful were they that both became celestial defenders of Israel.

For His work, God collected dust from all four corners of the world—red, white, black, yellow—so that no country could claim superiority over others, all had shared in the creation of man.

Why was man created alone? So that his descendants could claim superiority over each other.

This teaches another lesson: To kill a person is to destroy more than that person; to kill a person is to destroy all descendants that he might have had; to kill a person is to destroy mankind.

But man must not draw vanity from his destructive powers. Nor must he indulge in excessive pride for having been created at the hands of God. Man must be humble even though God was *very* pleased when he saw him. Why was man created last? So as not to become too arrogant, for even flies and mosquitoes could tell him: "We are older than you."

Yet the first man had good reasons to be proud. Not only had he heard God's voice and experienced the awesome mystery of his own beginnings, but he was also perfect. Everything about him was perfect: He was strong, handsome, wise, daring and just. His soul contained the souls of all his descendants. He was learned and innocent, good-hearted and obedient. No man will ever attain his perfection. Not even the Messiah? Yes, the Messiah will. But then the first man and the Messiah will be one.

He was—and remains—the crown of creation.

On the seventh day God rested. Thus rest, too, became part of creation. All of creation joined in that rest. Time became consecrated, sanctified. Shabbat: God's gift to man, a sanctuary in time. Israel's survival will be linked to it; Israel will keep Shabbat and Shabbat will keep Israel. If God is king, then Shabbat is His queen. And Israel is man's song of glory and gratitude to both.

Man was endowed with so many virtues and qualities that he could not but arouse jealousy among the angels. What was so special about him, they wanted to know. What made him worthy of so many privileges? So God decided that man ought to prove himself before the angels. All living creatures, were summoned to march past the angels. Can you name them? asked God. No, they could not. God turned to the first man. And you, can you? Yes, he could. And did. Evidently that was sufficient proof that man was wiser than the angels. Finally, God asked him: What is your name? The answer came instantly: Adam.

And because this was done last, man can possess anything in the world before he possesses himself.

Adam was living in Paradise with his wife, whom he called Eve. The way he came to know her is worth retelling. She wasn't Adam's idea, but God's. Adam was too lonely. Of all the living creatures, he alone had no mate. So God created a woman for him. But since Adam had seen how her body had been formed, he felt no desire for her. Which made God realize that man likes a woman to be somewhat mysterious. That is why he put Adam to sleep and carved her from one of his ribs. Thus, when Adam awoke from his first sleep, he was no longer alone. Eve was there with him.

Needless to emphasize the obvious: She was radiant with beauty and charm and intelligence. No woman will ever be as captivating.

Their wedding was performed in Paradise. God Himself officiated and angels surrounded the canopy, singing and dancing. The young couple received more gifts than any other in future times.

Strange, but the angels were no longer jealous of Adam. Was it because he now had a wife?

Adam and Eve were happy together—when they were together. They ran into trouble—when they were not.

When Adam was away, Eve held endless conversations with the serpent, who still resembled a human being. Food and sin were her favorite topics. Why did God forbid them to eat from the tree of knowledge and not from the tree of life? What made that tree so special? Eve discussed these questions with the serpent. She was curious and dissatisfied. "What precisely did God say?" the serpent asked her. "God told us that we could eat from every tree in the garden except the one standing in the middle; if we but touch that one, we shall die," replied Eve. This was not true and the serpent knew it. God had said nothing about touching the tree. Women tend to exaggerate and this can lead to disaster. What happened to Eve is a case in point.

"The reason for his prohibition is simple," said the serpent. "God is afraid—lest you become gods. Yes, Eve, should you and your husband eat from this tree, both of you shall become gods."

Though she was tempted, Eve managed to resist—she wanted to live and was afraid of God's punishment. But then the serpent pushed her against the tree provoking her: "You see, you touched the tree and you are alive. You may as well eat from it—nothing will happen to you." This time Eve could not resist. She ate from the tree. The serpent immediately went on to explain to Eve the consequences of her act: "Now you shall die and Adam will survive you, and tomorrow God will provide another woman for him to marry."

Of course, Eve grew jealous. And of course, she decided to do something—anything to make her husband share her fate. She tempted Adam, admittedly without much difficulty, and he too ate from the tree.

Once they had chosen knowledge over immortality, their eyes opened and they saw how naked they were—

and how vulnerable and fallible. And from that moment on, they lived with only their memories; they had left Paradise to enter history.

Eve kept asserting her superiority over Adam to the very end. Their first son—Cain—was named by her, not by him. The same was true of their second son—Abel. She foresaw the fate of the two brothers and told Adam about it. To prevent the murder, Adam separated them and made each choose a different occupation. Cain tilled the ground, Abel tended the sheep. Both were good, obedient children. They brought offerings to God, who accepted those of Abel but not those of his brother. This aroused Cain's hostility against his brother, a hostility climaxed by the first murder in history.

But there were many other reasons for this. Both had wanted to marry Abel's beautiful twin sister. And both had been determined to possess the ground upon which the Temple of Jerusalem was to be erected. Also, when Cain had felt rejected and humiliated by God, Abel had shown no compassion towards him. Cain had spoken to his brother and received no answer.

Cain's victory was by no means immediate. At first, when he threw himself on his brother, Abel managed to escape, running from hill to hill, from valley to valley, from one mountain to another. When Cain finally caught up with him, Abel resisted the assault and overpowered his brother. It was only when Cain begged for mercy that Abel, who was good-hearted, loosened his grip. That was the moment Cain had been waiting for. He jumped to his feet and slew his brother.

The lesson of all this? Pity is not always rewarded.

Questioned by God as to why he had committed the murder, Cain replied: First, how do you know? Who told you? Are there informers in heaven? Second, never having seen death before, how was I to know that I could kill? Third, why didn't you stop me? The thief who is caught inside the garden may well tell the guard: My trade is to steal and yours is to prevent me from stealing. I have done my work; why didn't you do yours? Why did you allow me inside the garden?

His arguments were sound, but still he was punished. He became a wanderer, finding peace nowhere. Once he met his father, now very old, and told him he had repented. That was when Adam composed his first song of praise to God.

Adam and Eve eventually had a third son named Seth —and we are all *his* descendants.

Cain was not the last human to commit sin. As more people inhabited the earth, more ways were found to displease God. They broke His laws, rejected His commandments, erred so far and fell so low that the Creator regretted His decision to bring the world into being.

Question: If man was guilty, why was it necessary to punish earth and all the other creatures? Answer: Imagine a man who, out of love for his son, arranges a huge celebration, invites the most distinguished guests and orders the most extraordinary dishes. But his son dies. So, the father sends everyone away and calls off the festivities. "I needed all this to make my son happy," he says, "now that he is dead, there is nothing I need."

As generations followed one another, His remorse kept growing. Even some of the angels strayed from the straight and narrow path. Having requested celestial permission to come and live on earth to teach humans respect for the law and love for God, they eventually allowed themselves to be corrupted—they took wives and had children. So decadent was mankind that it deserved only fallen angels. At the end of the tenth generation, God told Noah of His plan to wipe out all that mankind had built, so that He could start all over again.

Noah was the Just man of his times. Until the age of one hundred and twenty, he tried to convince his contemporaries to mend their ways. In vain. He warned them of future punishments. In vain. He told them of the coming flood, urging them to take precautionary measures. In vain. Even when he and his three sons began building their ark, the people refused to take him seriously; they laughed at him. Noah and his visions of horror, Noah and his nightmares. When they finally realized how foolish they had been, it was already too late. They were doomed. The animal world fared better, its representatives survived. Noah and his sons took care of the animal world with exemplary devotion; all year long they never closed an eye, looking after every beast, every animal, at all hours of the day and night.

So Noah watched as creation was destroyed. The floods lasted a whole year. When the rains came to a halt, Noah first sent a raven to see what was happening outside. Only the raven, having found a human corpse on the top of the mountain, began to devour it and forgot to return. Then Noah dispatched a dove to look around; the dove returned with the good news that it was safe now to leave the ark. But Noah had never disobeyed God; it was to please and obey God that he had built the ark, and had taken residence on it; in obedience to God he would leave it. Even when God ordered him back to land, Noah refused...unless God swore to him never again to use floods as punishment. Since God needed Noah to rebuild His universe, He gave him His pledge—which was fortunate because it was not long before Noah's own descendants chose to follow paths of sin.

No wonder Noah planted a vine and—miraculously—got drunk immediately!

There is a legend: While Noah was busy planting, Satan appeared before him and asked him what he was doing. "I am planting a vine," Noah answered. "What exactly is that?" "Its fruit is mellow and their juice gives cheer," Noah explained. "Would you like me to help you?" "Gladly," said Noah.

And so Satan took a lamb and sacrificed it in the vine; then he sacrificed a lion, then a monkey, then a pig. Finally he poured their blood together and sprinkled the vine with the mixture.

And so it is that when a man drinks one glass of wine he becomes gentle as a lamb. Two glasses and he takes himself for a lion. Three glasses and he begins to dance like a monkey. Four glasses will turn him into a pig, wallowing in dirt and apathy.

Headed by Nimrod, six hundred thousand men and women, all descendants of Noah's three sons, gathered in Babylonia and began erecting an immense tower that would touch the sky. So huge was the tower that it took a man a whole year to climb it. The work lasted many years and was done in a mood of constant excitement. People died, children were born: Nobody paid attention to anything except the work itself.

Nimrod's rebellion had three aims: Climb up into heaven and wage war against God; then replace Him with idols; and finally destroy His dwelling place.

Had the people been less united in their frenzy, God would have exterminated them. But their unity played in their favor, and obtained for them a lesser punishment.

God simply confused their language so that they could no longer communicate among themselves. When someone asked for mortar, his fellow worker handed him a brick—and what had once been a fervent, coherent community suddenly disintegrated. As did the tower itself. But the place where it once stood retains a special quality: Whoever steps on it forgets all he or she knows.

Abraham: A man for all seasons, endowed with all talents. His mission was to serve as God's messenger to man. Tradition rates him higher than Adam, whose errors he was asked to correct. Thanks to him, mankind was to survive destruction. Abraham: A merciful man who aroused compassion in God, and restored His faith in man.

Like Adam, Abraham was first in many areas: The first to be persecuted by earthly kings, the first refugee, the first rebel against organized society, the first believer and the first one to suffer for his belief, the first defender of man indicted by God: Abraham our forefather, our guide, our protector.

On the night he was born, a shiny new star appeared in the sky. King Nimrod saw it swallow up the four brightest stars and hover over the house of an idol-maker named Terah whose wife had just given birth to a son. To

King Nimrod this seemed a bad omen. The boy, if allowed to live, would outshine him and the four mightiest kings on earth. Therefore the boy must not live.

To protect his son from the king's henchman, Terah hid him in a mountain cave. For many years Abraham, in his loneliness, taught himself and meditated on life and its meaning. He attained truth with no one's help. In the beginning he saw the stars at night and loved their beauty: "They must be gods," he thought, and began to worship them. Then he watched the sun drive away the stars; he loved its warmth and power: "The sun is god," he thought and began worshipping it. Then clouds covered the sun, and Abraham understood his mistake and started to worship the clouds. But then winds dispersed the clouds and brought back the sun, and then the moon, and then the stars—and finally Abraham came to the conclusion that "There must be one ruler over creation as a whole—one God moves the sun and the moon and the stars and the winds. And He alone is to be praised and worshipped." As Abraham uttered his first prayer to God, a voice was heard in the depth of his heart, reverberating in the highest spheres: "*Hineni,* here I am, my son."

Thus, for the first time, God was God to man.

Once he had acquired the knowledge of God's existence, Abraham could have kept it to himself—but he did not. Quite the contrary: He spread it among his father's clients. Whenever one of them came to Terah's shop to purchase an idol, Abraham would admonish him: "Really, don't you think that at your age it is rather silly to worship a piece of wood or stone which was carved today?" That would have been enough to eventually ruin his father's business, but Abraham was impatient. Rather than wait for all the customers to visit the shop and listen to his sermons, he decided one day to smash all the idols on the shelves—leaving only the largest one intact. When Terah returned home, he wanted to know what happened. "Oh nothing," said Abraham. "The idols were hungry, so I fed them. But the big one got angry and killed all of them—so he could eat their food too." Terah looked at his son in disbelief: "Are you out of your mind? Don't you know that idols don't eat, don't quarrel, don't kill? Don't you know that they are lifeless?" At this, Abraham smiled: "Really, father? Then why worship them?"

Thus, Abraham succeeded in educating his own father.

However, he was unable to convert King Nimrod to his belief—which was unfortunate because it would have spared him many painful trials and tribulations. King Nimrod wanted him dead, and so he threw him into fiery ovens and empty pits, condemned him to hunger and despair, but time after time Abraham emerged unscathed. When there was nothing else left to learn from the persecutions, he left his native country and went to the land of Canaan where new adventures were awaiting him, and his descendants as well.

There, God made a covenant with him, saying: Your children's children will suffer but not forever; they will be oppressed but not forever; they will be strangers in strange lands but not forever—look at the sky, Abraham, can you count the stars? As plentiful shall your descendants be.

Abraham then fell asleep and in his sleep he saw a flaming torch and a burning furnace, illustrating the future suffering of Israel and also its mission—both being parts of the covenant.

Thus, whenever Jews suffer, they remind God of his covenant with Abraham and He reminds them of their mission.

Then came the episode of the sinful cities: Sodom and Gomorrah. God wanted them destroyed and Abraham interceded on their behalf: Do You intend to do away with the righteous and the wicked alike? Suppose there are but fifty Just men in Sodom? Or twenty? Or ten? Why should they perish? Will You, who are the Supreme Judge, act with injustice? Abraham's argument was logical but academic. The two cities were destroyed because there were no Just men in them.

Their inhabitants' sins were directed as much against mankind as against God. They lacked human warmth towards one another. They were inhospitable to strangers. Their judges were corrupt.

Travelers would be given gold and silver but not bread, and thus were driven to starvation. Then Sodomites would take back the gold and silver and rob the corpses of their belongings.

They were expert torturers. When a stranger arrived, he would be led to a bed of their invention. Six men would "help" him lie down. If he was too short for the bed, they would stretch him; if he was too long, they would press him inside. No visitor ever survived such a welcome.

Sodom and Gomorrah deserved their punishment —yet Abraham was right in trying to save them. If his pleas to God were credited to him as good deeds, it was because they were selfless. Unlike Job—who is often compared to Abraham—he argued with God not for his own sake but for others'.

Only Lot, Abraham's nephew, and his wife escaped the fires that swept through Sodom. But when they were advised not to look back, Lot obeyed, his wife did not. And—why not admit it?—our sympathy goes to her: How could Lot be so insensitive to the fate of his former friends and neighbors as to not even to cast a last glance backward? How could he not look back—one last time—at his own past? His wife seems to have been more human.

But her death was not Abraham's fault.

However it was partly *his* fault that another woman, his servant Haggar, and their son Ishmael had to leave his home and wander into the wilderness. He should have resisted Sarah. But Sarah was both jealous and sad, for she was barren and old and the sight of Haggar and her child increased her suffering; she felt humiliated, and her reaction was only human. What about Abraham? He obeyed an angel who told him to obey Sarah.

Actually, Sarah had no reason to despair, for soon after this she gave birth to a son. She named him Isaac: he will laugh. She was happy. So was her husband. But God was not.

For it came to pass that God decided to test again—for the tenth and the last time—his faithful servant Abraham. Take your son, your only son, the one you love, and bring him as an offering to me, He said. Abraham's answer was: "*Hineni*—here I am, ready and willing to fulfill your command."

Without making the slightest attempt to resist, to debate, to delay, to question or to understand the divine order, Abraham got up in the morning—while Sarah was still asleep—took his son and servants with him, and left in the direction of Mount Moriah.

For two days father and son said nothing to one another. Suddenly an old man appeared before Abraham; it was Satan in disguise. "Where are you heading?" he asked. "To prayer," said Abraham. "With a knife?" asked Satan. "With fire and wood? Nobody goes to prayer like that." "Well, we may have to stay a while," said Abraham. "A day or two. We may have to slaughter a lamb and build a fire to roast it."

At that point Satan dropped his mask and exclaimed: "Poor man with your poor tales...Don't you know that I was there—in heaven—when the order was given?" Abraham did not reply. "But tell me," Satan continued, "tell me old man, did you lose your mind, your heart? Do you really intend to sacrifice your son, given to you at the age of one hundred?" "Yes, I do," said Abraham. "But tomorrow, old fool, tomorrow God may demand more sacrifices, even more cruel ones, will you obey them too?" "Yes, I will," said Abraham. "But then He may accuse *you* of murder..." "Even so, I am not to question His will or His intentions," said Abraham.

Powerless with the father, Satan tried his luck with the son, to whom he appeared in the disguise of a young boy: "Where are you going?" he asked him. "To study the Torah," said Isaac. "Now or after?" "After what?" "After your death," said Satan. "What a silly question," said Isaac. "Don't you know the Torah is given to the living alone?" "Poor son of a poor woman," said Satan. "For years and years she has lived in hope and prayer to give birth to you and now—this old father is going to kill you..."

As Isaac refused to believe him, Satan continued: "Listen, you will die and brother Ishmael will get all the beautiful gifts that are meant to be yours."

Now Isaac was somewhat shaken. He turned to Abraham and asked: "Is it true? Am I going to die?" "Pay no attention to what he says," Abraham replied.

Then Satan, determined to shake Abraham's faith, used the most dangerous weapon of all: Truth. Discarding his disguises, he revealed his secret: I am not human and I am not from here, I come from the other side and this is what I heard over there: All this is nothing but a test, Isaac will survive and the lamb will be offered in his place.

Still, Abraham paid no attention to his words. He continued to climb Mount Moriah with Isaac at his side. They were together now more than ever before. Together they reached the place, together they prepared the altar. Abraham behaved like a father preparing his son's wedding and Isaac like a groom building his own wedding canopy. Both were serene and at peace with themselves and with each other. Then, suddenly Isaac felt fear. "Father," he said, "what will you and mother do afterward?" Abraham looked straight into his eyes. And he wept. And his tears fell into the eyes of Isaac.

But the slaughter was averted. An angel's voice was heard: "Lay not thy hand upon the boy." Why did an angel intervene and not God? We are taught by this that God alone may order man to kill, but to save lives, the angel's authority is sufficient.

A ram was sacrificed in Isaac's stead. And Abraham returned to his servants down below. But, he returned—alone.

What happened to Isaac? Some sources say that he went to study in the *yeshiva* of Shem and Eber, Isaac's ancestors. Others believe he went up to heaven where he composed the prayer of the resurrection of the dead. One thing is certain: He was not with Abraham when Abraham came to join his servants. Something had happened between father and son—their relationship was no longer the same.

For one thing, Sarah was no longer alive. While the trial was taking place, Satan had visited Sarah and given her a detailed description of the events at Mount Moriah. The shock had been too great for the old mother. She died before her husband and son returned.

She was the real victim. With Sarah gone, the holy cloud that had hovered over the family's tent disappeared. It reappeared only when Isaac married Rebecca, who was as worthy as Sarah and as pious and compassionate as she.

Life went on. Isaac was raising a family of his own. And Abraham's last day drew near. Sent by God to tell Abraham to prepare himself, the angel was unable to accomplish his mission for "Abraham is unique—no one is as righteous, as hospitable, as truthful as he." Yet Abraham deserved to know that his day was near—so God composed a dream for Isaac in which he saw the sad event happen. When Isaac began to weep, so did Abraham, and so did the Angel—and Abraham felt his soul leaving him—as in a dream.

Rebecca, daughter of Bethuel the Aramean and sister of Laban, was fourteen when she was married to Isaac. The matchmaker was Eliezer, Abraham's faithful servant, whose virtues were so great that he entered Paradise alive.

What made Eliezer choose Rebecca? Her kindness. Of all the maidens present at the well, she alone offered him and his camels water. Aware of the honor that had been bestowed upon her, she consented immediately to follow Eliezer and travel to meet her husband-to-be. Miracles occurred during that journey, which lasted but three hours instead of seventeen days. Rebecca found Isaac in the middle of his *minha* prayers—which he had authored— and this is how we forever imagine him: In prayer.

They had two children—Jacob and Esau, who quarreled even before their birth. Whenever Rebecca walked by a pagan temple, Esau would move in her womb. Whenever she passed a House of Study, Jacob would move around. Their quarrels lasted their entire lifetime and beyond. What were they quarreling about? Some say it was about the meaning of life and death. Others say it was about the importance of the present world versus that of the world to come. Jacob believed in man's immortality, Esau did not. "Noah was righteous, has he reappeared...?" Esau asked his brother. "Our grandfather Abraham was righteous, has he reappeared...?" Esau asked his brother. Yet Jacob went on believing and Esau went on mocking him. Finally, Esau sold his brother his birthright for a plate of lentils. Why for so little? That was Esau's way of turning the event into a farce. For him, all life was a farce. It had to be, since he could take it away from living creatures—including human beings; on the day Esau sold his birthright, he had slain three men.

No wonder that Rebecca favored Jacob—so shy, so modest, so vulnerable! Why did Isaac favor Esau? Because Isaac was blind? Because Isaac wanted to compensate for injustices done to his own older brother? Whatever the reason, Isaac intended to give his blessings to Esau, not to Jacob. And Rebecca and Jacob cunningly managed to confuse the two sons' identities and fool the blind old man. When Esau realized he had been cheated, he shed three tears—and because of his grief, Jacob's children and theirs are still suffering in exile.

Were it not for this subterfuge, we would all be Esau's descendants, not Jacob's. Still, it may be better to be the heir of a liar than the heir of a killer.

Esau did not kill Jacob, though he hated him even more than before. He did not kill Jacob because their father was still alive. But what if Esau were to have a change of heart? Rebecca decided it would be safer to have Jacob stay out of sight. She sent him away to Haran to spend time with her brother Laban.

Jacob, who had never been alone before, spent his first night in fear. He had a dream in which he saw a ladder whose upper rungs reached into heaven. Angels were ascending and descending, each one representing a great nation, illustrating the notion that earthly victories are, as such, temporary. Frightened, he cried out: Does this mean that Israel, too, will rise and then disappear? And he prayed to God and God told him not to be afraid. Though the Temple might be destroyed, Israel would live forever.

Unlike his father, Jacob had many earthly ties. He worked, he made deals, he showed concern for food and clothing. He ate and slept regularly—which is natural. Yet it makes him different from those who went before. He seems to us more human. Weaker.

A Talmudic parable: The angels saw Jacob's image in heaven and were impressed by its light and purity; so they came down to earth to meet him in person—and found him asleep.

There came a time when Jacob did not sleep at all, for the next twenty years—while he stayed with his uncle Laban. He worked hard during the days and recited Psalms during the nights—all the while thinking of Rachel...

It had been love at first sight. From the moment he noticed Rachel standing near the well, he saw no one else. He kissed her—as is the custom among cousins—and cried, so moved was he by her beauty. One commentator has a more down-to-earth interpretation: He cried because he was poor and empty-handed, and had nothing to offer Rachel and her father. That Laban was disappointed is clear. He could not believe that Isaac's son would come without some kind of gifts. "It is true," Jacob told him. "I have neither money nor precious stones; all I have are words."

Still Laban kept his nephew in his house, for that was the advice he had received from his idols. Eventually, Jacob married both of Laban's daughters: First Leah, then Rachel. Jacob paid for them with his labor. He cared little for Leah but he loved Rachel. By the time that the two sisters had given him twelve children, the last two Rachel's—Jacob felt it was time to leave Laban and return to the land of his childhood.

This was no easy project. Laban wanted to keep Jacob, whose labor cost him nothing. He also was opposed to his daughters and grandchildren going away so far—probably for good.

So Jacob decided to leave under the cover of night. Predictably, Laban reacted with outrage and anger; he was ready to kill his son-in-law. Luckily, Laban too had a dream, in which he was warned not to harm Jacob lest he too would die. Nonetheless Laban gathered together his friends and pursued the fugitive, whom he eventually found in the midst of prayer. He questioned Jacob at length: Why had he left as a thief in the night? Jacob denied any wrongdoing: He had never stolen anything, he had worked hard and had been scrupulously loyal to his employer. The argument ended in a treaty between the two men. They parted in friendship, the Aramean returning to his homeland and Jacob to his.

However, Jacob was not out of danger. Quite the contrary: Only now did the threat against him become real. Incited by Laban, Esau's old hatred for his brother was revived and he made plans to kill Jacob.

Though he was protected by six hundred thousand angels, Jacob was frightened. At first he tried to placate his brother by sending to Esau emissaries with all kinds of gifts and words of reason and friendship. "Why do you wish to kill me...?" he asked, "because I received our father's blessings in your place? They didn't do me much good. I have had to work hard for every head of cattle I own. So you are wrong to envy me. The sun shines on both my land and yours—and the rain falls as well on both. Our father blessed me with the dew of heaven, but he blessed you with the fertility of the earth. Please do stop envying me."

The emissaries returned to Jacob and told him of the failure of their missions. In spite of the presents and the friendly gestures, in spite of his self-deprecating words, Esau still wanted Jacob dead.

Jacob's fear increased. Why did he feel that he could not rely on God's promise to bring him back in peace to his father's home? Because Jacob wondered whether God had not, after all, decided to favor Esau who, unlike himself, lived in the Holy Land and, unlike himself, could fulfill the commandment of honoring one's parents by serving them. Another commentator goes further: Jacob's fear was twofold; he was afraid that he would be killed *or* that he would have to kill. Victory was as unnatural to him as defeat; as far as his relations with his brother were concerned, he wanted neither.

When war seemed unavoidable, Jacob decided to face the conflict alone. He sent his family to the other side of the river Jabbok. Then the long waiting began. He wanted—and needed—to be alone with himself, alone with his memories. He was finally about to meet the lost brother with whom he had been obsessed for twenty years—when they had last faced and fought one another, in the presence of their blind father.

What had happened to Esau in those twenty years? What happened to himself? Had they changed much?

On the river Jabbok and its shores, night had fallen.

Then, all of a sudden, Jacob sensed that he was no longer alone. Someone was there behind him, near him—inside him?—watching him, waiting for the opportunity to assault him.

Who was it? Assuredly a stranger—but a stranger sent by whom and for what purpose? One commentator says he was Esau's guardian. Another believes, on the contrary, that it was Jacob's guardian. If so, why did they fight? Because the angel meant to prepare him for the next day's critical encounter with Esau.

Anyway, whether friend or foe, the angel wrestled with Jacob the whole night and the dust underneath them whirled up in shapes so huge they rose to God's throne. And though the angel was as big as a third of the whole world, Jacob had the upper hand. Because of this, the angel encouraged him by saying: "Look how strong I am and yet you defeated me—why then should you worry about Esau? You will defeat him, too." Still, Jacob did not emerge from the struggle unharmed. He was left limping, wounded by the angel. One does not wrestle, even with one's own angel, with impunity.

At dawn, the angel said: "Let me go, for dawn is breaking." Jacob, not satisfied with his victory, refused, asking: "Are you afraid of daylight? Are you a thief or a gambler?" The angel grew desperate: "Let me go for I am expected by my companions to sing our praise to God." "On one condition," said Jacob. "You must bless me first —then you may go."

"Why?" asked the angel. "You are the son and I am the servant—who is more important? The servant needs the blessing more than the son."

"True," said Jacob, "but when the angels left Abraham, they gave him their blessing."

"Yes—but they were sent for that purpose, I was not."

Why didn't Jacob, at that point, ask him the purpose of his mission? Evidently, the blessing was more important to him than an answer. In the end he received what he wanted. The angel gave him his blessing in the form of a name. Thus Jacob became Israel—for he had fought with an angel of God and won.

That same night, Michael was appointed as the eternal guardian of the people of Israel.

The encounter between the two enemy brothers was anti-climactic: They embraced and wept. They had expected the worst—a definitive test of life and death—and had managed to avoid it. They behaved, instead, like brothers. Forgotten was the old hatred, forgotten the resentment from long ago. They shed tears of reconciliation.

Nevertheless, some commentators find it difficult to present Esau in so favorable a light. They prefer to think of him as being cunning to the bitter end. He embraced Jacob? Only because he wanted to bite Jacob's neck— which God turned into ivory so that Esau broke his teeth. *That* was why he wept. He refused to receive Jacob's presents? Even while refusing them with words, he was reaching out with his hands, demanding them.

Jacob gave him pearls, precious stones and one-tenth of his cattle. But the animals refused to go with Esau and ran away. Only those who were too weak to escape remained. If Esau was disappointed, he didn't show it. He had learned his lesson: Jacob was protected by heaven; watched over by an army of angels. It was better to leave him alone.

Esau was a practical person—but so was Jacob. From his behavior in this chapter, we learn the three attitudes adopted later by the Jewish people whenever they faced the threats of a powerful enemy. First, Jacob prayed to God. Then, he tried to soothe Esau with good words and expensive presents. Third—being left no choice—he made the necessary preparations for battle.

But this time there had been no need for battle.

Once he was back in the Land of Canaan, Jacob thought he could begin to lead a peaceful existence. He was wrong. New suffering was awaiting him, in the person of his favorite son, Joseph, whom he loved too much—and too publicly....

Not only was Joseph the oldest son of his favorite wife, Rachel, but he also resembled Jacob—just as Isaac had resembled Abraham. Thus Jacob felt closest to him. Joseph received the most expensive presents and the most secret teachings: Whatever Jacob had learned in the famous yeshiva of Shem and Eber, he transmitted to Joseph.

No wonder that the other brothers grew jealous. Moreover, he gave them other excellent reasons, for not only was he his father's favorite, he often boasted about it. Joseph painted his eyes, combed his hair with great care and walked with a provocative gait, doing everything he could to attract attention. Worse: He was a gossip, playing friend against friend, father against child.

He must have felt so secure in his position that he would not hesitate to tell his brothers of a dream he had had: "You gathered fruit and so did I, but yours bowed to mine." They refused to listen, but he continued in the same vein, going even further. Joseph told them—in the presence of their father—of another dream he had had: The sun, the moon and eleven stars had bowed before him. Surely that was too much even for his father, who rebuked him, hoping thus to divert the other brothers' envy from Joseph. In vain. They had made up their minds to do away with their brother.

So one day, as Joseph was sent by Jacob to see his brothers in the field, they seized him and cast him into a pit of snakes.

Question: Why did Jacob send him there? Didn't he know how the brothers felt about him? Didn't he consider how perilous the mission would be for his beloved son? One commentator says: Yes, Jacob knew, but couldn't imagine that his own children would do such a thing. Another says: Jacob was afraid that a war had broken out between the people of Shechem and his children—and he had dispatched Joseph to go and report back to him whether his fears were justified or not.

In fact, they were. Only this particular war was taking place between his own sons.

It was a war in which everyone concerned was a loser.

The day on which Joseph was sold as a slave marked the beginning of Israel's exile; its darkness outweighs that of the day on which the Temple was destroyed.

It had been Judah's idea. He meant thus to save his brother's life; better to live like a slave than die young. But, states the Talmud, Judah is not to be praised; he should have fought for Joseph's freedom and dignity, not only for his life. He should not have settled for halfway solutions. There are situations which brook no compromise.

The Midianites paid twenty pieces of silver for their slave, enough for a pair of shoes for each of the brothers. Why shoes and not bread? The brothers declared: "We cannot eat with this money, which is the price for our brother's blood, but we shall tread upon him instead—thus shall we prove that his dreams of superiority were naught."

The Midianites soon sold him to some Ishmaelites. Joseph overheard the latter saying that they were heading toward Egypt and so he wept bitterly. His new master, tired of his lamentations, dealt him painful blows. From these he cried even more, for he knew that with every step he took, he moved farther and farther from his father. But nothing could compare to his wailing when he reached his mother's grave in Ephrath. There he threw himself to the ground crying: "Arise, mother, come and see how your son has been sold into slavery with no one to pity him. Awake, mother, and weep with me over my misfortune... Arise, mother and accuse my brothers before God and see whom He will justify and whom He will find guilty." He cried and cried for hours until he lay exhausted on the grave. Then he heard a voice, his mother's, comforting him: "I saw your tears, my son Joseph, and I know your misery. I am grieved for your sake and your grief adds to my own. But you must put your trust in God. He is with you. He will deliver you from all evil."

Joseph broke out in renewed tears and the Ishmaelites beat him with renewed vigor until God sent darkness to envelop them. The earth began to tremble, the sky was cut by lightning. All creatures trembled with fear. And the Ishmaelites understood that they were wrong in torturing their slave and decided to quickly get rid of him—which they did as soon as they entered the land of Egypt. A local nobleman named Potiphar bought Joseph for four hundred pieces of silver—which made the slave-merchants doubly happy, for the deal was a profitable one.

Though Jacob's sons repented immediately after their deed, they did not tell him the truth. A wild beast must have devoured Joseph, they told him. "Go and find it," Jacob ordered them. "Take your swords and your bows and bring me the first beast you catch. Perhaps it will be the one that killed my child. Perhaps he will be avenged."

The sons obeyed their inconsolate father. They went into the wilderness and caught a wolf, whom Jacob seized with anger and sorrow: "Why did you tear my son to pieces?" he asked the beast. "Did you have no fear of God in your heart? Didn't you know what grief you would cause me, his father? Why did you devour my son without reason?" To Jacob's surprise, the wolf opened his mouth and spoke: "Let God who created you, and your soul which keeps you alive, be my witnesses that I have not seen your son; I have not killed him. I came from far away searching for my own young whose fate is similar to your son's. He vanished ten days ago and I went forth to find him. While I was searching for him, I was seized by your sons. That is my story." Jacob set the wolf free and continued to mourn for Joseph as before.

He alone was mourning. Everyone else around him knew that Joseph had not been killed by a wild beast but rather sold as a slave. And that he was alive. Isaac, too, who was endowed with the gift of prophecy, knew. But they were all sworn to secrecy—as was God himself. They all knew and they all kept silent.

Both Potiphar and his wife loved their young slave. But Potiphar had been rendered "harmless" by the angel Gabriel. His wife was not; she pursued Joseph relentlessly and senselessly. Yet Joseph resisted her to the end.

In the beginning she tried to draw him to her by treating him as her so-called adopted son—since she had no son of her own. Joseph prayed to God on her behalf and lo and behold, she bore a son. Then she tried to seduce him—and refused, she threatened him with torture and death. In vain. She even went so far as to offer to forsake idol worship and convert to his religion. In vain. At one point she threatened to commit suicide. He talked her out of it, but remained distant and aloof.

Still she pursued him, paying him compliments, praising his eyes, his hair, while he chided her and told her to pay more attention to her household. Finally, one time, when Joseph refused to look at her, she had iron shackles placed under his chin, forcing him to keep his head high all the time and look her in the face.

One day, when everybody in Egypt was taking part in a public celebration, Joseph found himself alone in the house—alone with Potiphar's wife. On that day she appeared to him in all her beauty—and indeed she was the most beautiful woman in Egypt. She stood before him naked, filled with lust. And for one moment he too was overcome by desire. He too undressed. But the image of his father appeared before his eyes and made him regain his senses. "My friend, my love, what happened?" the puzzled woman wanted to know. "I see my father," he explained. "But where? Where is he? We are alone in the house." "No," he replied. "We are not alone. But you belong to a people that cannot see. I belong to a people that can and does."

The rejected woman managed to turn the story around and make it appear as though Joseph had assaulted her. Whether her husband believed her or not is not clear. Talmudic sources try, successfully, to prove both hypotheses... What *is* clear is that Joseph ended up in jail and stayed there ten years.

Now he had paid for his youthful sins, now he deserved to be called Joseph the pious or Joseph the just.

New experiences, new encounters awaited him in jail. Having gone through so much at so young an age, he knew how to get along with people—all kinds of people. The warden assigned various duties to him, duties which put him in touch with important inmates, including the king's former chief butler and chief baker. Joseph would listen to their tales and interpret their dreams—some cheerful and others disturbing. Was his a keen sense of psychology or a divinely induced intuition? Whatever the explanation, he knew how to foretell the future. And since Pharao had dreams of his own waiting for someone to decipher their meaning, Joseph was brought before him.

Pharao's dreams are known, and Joseph read them correctly. The seven fat cows, the seven lean ones. The fat years and the lean years. A dreamer himself, Joseph had no difficulty in discovering the key to Pharao's nightly visions. His deductive and descriptive talents were so impressive that it was only natural for the king to keep him at his side. Thus Joseph made the stunning leap from prisoner to Viceroy in less than one day.

His inauguration was celebrated throughout the kingdom with the participation of a thousand musicians, five thousand warriors and forty thousand noblemen. Hundreds and hundreds of women stood at their windows, throwing him their rings and bracelets, hoping to draw his attention, but he did not even look up.

His thoughts were free of lust, his feelings free of desire. Whether in jail or in a royal palace, Joseph remained Joseph.

When his prophecies came true, Joseph's position became very strong. He not only controlled Egypt's national economy, but its police as well. No one could enter or leave the country without his knowledge which is what he wanted. He wanted to know exactly when, among all those arriving to buy grain, there would be his brothers from Canaan. And though they entered through separate gates—obeying their father's orders not to arouse suspicion by coming as a group—their arrival was reported to Joseph.

He had them arrested as spies. Why? Why did he play games with his father's children? Was this his way of seeking revenge? And if so, was this proper behavior? How does vengeance fit into the Jewish tradition? How is it compatible with its teaching?

One commentator maintains that Joseph must still have been suspicious of his brothers' motives—and for good reasons. An angel had warned him that "They have come to kill you." But most commentators prefer to rehabilitate the brothers: Their purpose, it is said, was not only to buy grain but also—and mainly—to find their brother and bring him back home to their grief-stricken father.

That was why they had not behaved like other foreigners purchasing food for their hungry families. They did not go straight to the grain markets. Instead, they first roamed around the streets and marketplaces. They even went to establishments of ill-repute; indeed, that was where they had been seized by the Egyptian police.

Denying the charges of spying, they tried to convince

the Viceroy of their honorable intentions. Long ago, they had a brother who disappeared; they hoped to find him here. "Why here?" asked Joseph. "Have you looked everywhere else in the world? Is Egypt the last country on your list?" "We heard that some Ishmaelites stole him and sold him here as a slave. And since he was resplendent with beauty, we thought that he might have been sold for shameful purposes. That is why your agents found us *there*..." Joseph pressed them further: "Suppose you find him and he is a slave—would you buy him back?" "Yes, we would." "Suppose his master refuses to sell him, what would you do then?" "We would kill the master and free our brother." "Is that why you came here? To kill the inhabitants of this kingdom?" He ordered them jailed—which was good for their souls for they thus expiated the sins which they had committed both against their brother and their father.

Still, as far as Joseph was concerned, the game was not over. He intended to show his brothers that what they had done to him, they were capable of doing unto each other. At one point, he expressed the wish of seeing their youngest brother—Benjamin—whom Jacob had kept at home. So he sent them back and, to make sure of their return, he kept one of them—Simon—as a hostage. Simon pleaded with them not to abandon him: "Are you going to do with me as you did with Joseph?" he cried. "What can we do?" they replied in despair, "Our families need us. We must go and bring them food, lest they perish of hunger."

Seventy strong Egyptians were ordered by their viceroy to bind Simon—but they could not. He simply shouted at them and they fell to the ground, crushed, with broken teeth. Only Joseph's son Manasseh was able to carry out the order. With one blow, he disarmed Simon, who was so astonished that he exclaimed: "This blow was dealt not by an Egyptian but by one of ours."

And so we see that, in times of peril, the real threat lies within ourselves.

At first Jacob refused to comply with the Egyptian viceroy's request. But as food ran out, and his grandchildren stared at him with hungry faces, he began to have second thoughts. It was Judah's argument that finally made him yield: "If Benjamin comes with us," Judah said, "he may or may not be taken away by the Egyptian king. But one thing is certain: If he stays here we will all die of hunger."

The resigned father then wrote a long, detailed letter "From Jacob, son of Isaac, grandson of Abraham, Prince of God, to the mighty and wise king, ruler of Egypt— peace." He described the situation of his family—the famine that had ravaged the land of Canaan. "I was informed of the accusations made against my sons and I hereby declare that they are innocent. I am the one who told them to use different gates... I am the one who ordered them to go everywhere and look for Joseph...."

Once again, the brothers left for Egypt. Jacob stayed home. More than ever, worried. More than ever, alone.

Joseph staged every element of the reunion with his brothers with great dramatic skill. His first meeting with Benjamin. His way of concealing his emotions. Only when he held his father's letter in his hand did he come close to tears. He had to leave the room to go and weep outside, alone.

Why did he then invite all his brothers to a festive Sabbath meal? Why did he continue to build suspense by having a cup planted in Benjamin's saddle? Why the elaborate play-acting that allowed them to go away, only to bring them back again? Only to show that Benjamin, too, was expendable to them? To drive them to beat Benjamin as they did Joseph long ago? One commentator answers in the affirmative. The brothers did call Benjamin a thief, they did deal him blows, they did act out once more their sin towards Joseph. And, he adds, they did all this so as to repent with greater sincerity.

In fact, says the Talmud, they all did agree to give up Benjamin—only Judah refused. Facing the Viceroy in open defiance, he said: "From the very beginning, you did everything to embarrass us. Many people from many countries come here to buy grain and none is questioned about their family relations as we were. Did we come to marry your daughter or offer you our sister in marriage? No. Yet you asked us questions and questions and none were left unanswered...." "You talk so much, too much," said Joseph. "Your brothers keep quiet and you talk— why? Why you." "Because I am responsible for Benjamin's return. I promised it to my father." "But you had no such worries when you sold your brother for twenty pieces of silver," said Joseph. "You lied to your father, you told him that a wild beast had devoured his son. You were not afraid of causing him grief then, yet Joseph was innocent of no crime while Benjamin is guilty of theft. Go and tell your father that the rope has followed the water bucket."

A shattered Judah cried out: "I cannot return to my father without his youngest son, I cannot!" And his outcry was so powerful that the whole land shook, destroying the cities of Pithom and Raamses, which remained in ruins until they were rebuilt by the Israelites one generation later. Judah and his brothers were ready to destroy the entire kingdom. It was saved, though, when Joseph finally decided to make himself known to his brothers; he did not wish to let any more innocent people suffer as a result of his game.

The brothers could only be amazed when the inquisitive ruler changed his tone of voice and, switching to Hebrew, said: "Your brother, the one that you sold? *I* bought him... Yes, I am going to call him and he will be here... And you will see him for yourselves." And raising his voice, he called out: "Joseph, come! Come Joseph, son of Jacob, come and meet your brothers!"

Judah, Simon and the others turned their eyes in all-directions looking, staring, waiting.... But nobody appeared through the door.

"Why look there?" asked the viceroy. "Look at me—I am Joseph, your brother!"

So great was their shock that they died on the spot. But God, in His mercy, revived them—on the spot.

They stared at him with disbelief: When last they had seen him, he had been young and poor and defenseless. Now he was mature and rich and powerful.

When they were at last persuaded that he was indeed their lost brother whom they had betrayed, they were overcome by shame and also by fear—what would stop him from taking revenge? In desperation, they threw themselves at him with the intent to kill him. Fortunately, an angel intervened and saved Joseph from death, and the brothers from committing the irreparable.

Joseph was not angry. On the contrary, he tried to soothe their wounded feelings: "You mustn't be sad or angry. There was a purpose in what you did long ago. I was meant to come here: I was sent by God to save lives."

And they all wept and wept—for themselves and even more for their descendants.

Joseph sent his brothers to bring Jacob to Egypt: "Tell him of the honors that are mine here." A question: Is it conceivable that Joseph was boasting? The answer: Joseph wanted his father to know that the honors had had no effect on him—he had remained the same.

What if his father did not believe that it was he? "Tell him that the last time we were together, he taught me the law of the heifer whose neck is broken in the valley."

And so Jacob answered Joseph's call. As father and son embraced and wept with joy, Jacob was quietly whispering the prayer: *Shma Israel,* Hear, O Israel.

Now—for the first time—the whole family, united at last, lived in peace and happiness.

Their happiness lasted seventeen years. Then, when Jacob felt that death was near, he summoned his children around his bed to give them his last blessings. He warned them not to fight among themselves, "For unity is the principal prerequisite for Israel's redemption." He had planned to reveal to them the awesome mystery of *achrit hayamim*—the end of time—but the *Shekhina*—the divine presence—left him and he saw nothing. Jacob wondered whether this was because of him or his children. Who among them was unworthy of ultimate knowledge?

Whose faith was tainted? To reassure him, his children proclaimed the *Shma Israel* in unison: "Hear O Israel, God is our God, God is one." As a reward, each of them received a fragment of the hidden knowledge of the Messianic era to come.

Like his father Isaac and his grandfather Abraham, Jacob died in peace. His soul was not taken by the Angel of death but by the *Shekhina*—the divine presence—who came to claim it with a kiss.

In accordance with Jacob's wish, Joseph arranged for his father's body to be taken to Canaan for burial.

Jacob was placed upon a couch of ivory, covered with purple drapery, studded with gold and gems. He was surrounded by his sons wrapped in sackcloth, and his casket was followed by princes of the families of Esau and Ishmael and mourned by the men and women of Egypt. More important, the *Shekhina* herself accompanied the procession that continued for seventeen days until the body was interred in the cave of Machpela, in Hebron, where an empty place was waiting for the last of the patriarchs to come and rest.

Because Joseph so respectfully and faithfully carried out Jacob's last wish, he was rewarded by God. When the children of Israel left Egypt, they took his body along to Canaan. And Moses himself made all the arrangements for his burial.

And Jacob's children knew happiness and prosperity in their new country; they were respected and liked. Until, suddenly, things changed: For no apparent reason people began to fear them. And envy them. And finally hate them. Suddenly, people found them too rich, too numerous, too powerful.

When the Egyptians were drawn into a terrible war, they won only after the intervention of the people of Israel. That, too, they could not forgive. Still, as long as even one of Jacob's children was alive, nobody dared attack the people of Israel. At the death of Levi, the last surviving son, there came an abrupt change. Particularly since it coincided with the ascension to the throne of a new king who preferred to forget Joseph's good deeds.

The rest is well known.

The first anti-Jewish measures. The forced labor. The humiliations. The women performing men's heavy labor, the men performing women's tasks; all measures meant to demonstrate the uselessness of their suffering. The edict forbidding the slaves to sleep in their homes so as to prevent conjugal love. The murder of male infants, the crime which finally provoked God to make his presence known.

And this is how it came to pass: An angel seized an infant about to be walled-in alive and brought him before God who, grief-stricken, remembered the promise He had made to Abraham, Isaac and Jacob. In this incident began the events which culminated in the Exodus. Moses became His messenger.

From the moment of his birth, Moses' life was touched by miracles. Floating down the Nile's waters, an angel made him cry at the opportune moment so as to be heard by Batya, Pharoa's daughter. Moved by compassion, she brought him back to the palace and entrusted him to a wet-nurse—who, unbeknownst to all—was the infant's own mother.

Once, when Moses was three, while playing on Pharao's knees, he reached up and, taking the crown off Pharao's head, placed it on his own. "An evil omen," cried the king's counselors, "you must kill him, for he craves your throne and your kingdom!" By a stroke of luck, an angel assumed the countenance of a sage attached to the court and counseled moderation. "Let us see if this child is just a child," he said, "let us place before him two dishes, one containing glowing coals and the other precious stones and jewels. If the child reaches for the jewels, we shall know that he knows what he wants. If, on the other hand, he touches the coals, we shall know that his deeds are unrelated to any plan."

The two dishes were placed before the child. Moses' hands went out toward the jewels but the angel moved them toward the coals, which burned his tongue—but saved his life.

At the palace, Moses received an education suitable for a prince. Tutors were brought in from far-away lands to teach him the sciences and the arts. His intelligence was such that he soon surpassed his teachers. Whether or not he maintained relations with his persecuted brethren, the sources do not reveal. If we are to give them credence, Moses was already an adolescent by the time he met them. He was touched by their sorrow and grieved for their misfortune. And he began to help them.

First, he obtained permission from the king to let his brethren rest on the day of the Sabbath. Then he pleaded with them not to lose hope, telling them that "Clouds are always followed by sunshine; and after a storm there always is calm.... You'll see. There shall be better times for you."

And then God said to him: "Since you have left your palace to take care of the children of Israel who are your brothers, I shall forsake my occupations in heaven and on earth in order to converse with you."

Moses was becoming more and more involved in the lives of the slaves, protecting them more and more every day. One day he came upon an Egyptian overseer striking a Hebrew foreman and became so enraged that he killed the overseer on the spot.

In so doing, says the Talmud, he performed an act of justice. Having raped the foreman's wife, the overseer had planned to simply eliminate the husband, whose wrath he feared. He had begun to strike the Hebrew when Moses, who knew everything, threw himself on him, shouting: "Was it not enough for you to rape his wife? Now you want to kill him, too?" And at the same time Moses addressed himself to God: "You promised Abraham that his children would be as plentiful as the stars—and You do nothing to save them? But if all are exterminated, what will You do with Your Law?"

Then Moses pronounced the name of God and the Egyptian fell down—dead.

There came a time when he almost regretted his act. Observing two Hebrews quarreling, almost coming to blows, he said to the one: "Rasha, evil one, why are you striking your brother?" The answer came back instantly: "What is it to you? Do you by any chance want to kill us too—just as you killed the Egyptian?"

From this incident Moses understood that the affair had become public knowledge and concluded that perhaps his own life now was in danger.... But, who could have talked? Who could have informed on Moses? There had been only three eyewitnesses: The Egyptian, Moses and the foreman Moses had wished to save. Therefore, an Egyptian being dead, the informer could have been only —the foreman himself....

Moses was arrested, tried and condemned to death. But the angel Michael assumed the executioner's face and the executioner took on Moses' face. Thus Moses was able to escape. Pharao sent troops in pursuit, but the pursuers were all struck deaf, dumb and blind: Thus, those who knew where Moses had found shelter were unable to speak of it, and those who could speak knew nothing. The flight was dramatic, filled with spectacular adventures. Ethiopia was in a state of war when he arrived there at the age of twenty-seven. He soon became its king and kept his throne for forty years. Then he took to the road once more and eventually settled in Midian, where he married the daughter of the priest Jethro and from then on led the peaceful life of a shepherd.

One day, he saw a sheep leaving the flock. He ran after it and found it near a stream: "I didn't know that you were thirsty," said Moses. "You must be terribly tired after running like this." He shouldered the creature and carried it back to the flock. And God said to him: "Since you are capable of such compassion toward a flock that belongs to a mortal, I shall entrust My own flock to you."

Soon after, Moses saw what no one else could see.

From the distance he saw, at the foot of Mount Horeb, a very unusual bush; though it was burning and burning, it was not consumed by the flames. And though there were other shepherds nearby, he alone saw the fire and heard the voice calling him, turning him into the messenger.

Why did God choose to appear in a bush? As a token of his modesty. And also as a reminder of the symbolic aspect of divine intervention: the bush is Israel. Just as birds cannot fly through the bush without being scratched by the thorns, the enemies of Israel shall not attack this small people without being wounded.

Moses was ordered to return to Egypt to liberate his people. He refused. Why? Excessive humility. For seven days and seven nights God tried to persuade him not to refuse the mission—and finally He succeeded. Moses accepted with one condition: That God agree to grant his every wish. God agreed, but made two exceptions: Moses would not be allowed to enter the Promised Land or to escape death.

In exchange, every time Moses would ask God to forgive the trespasses of His people, the request would be granted.

Moses took his wife and two sons and started on the road to Egypt. At nightfall they stopped to rest at an inn. There, Moses was attacked by an angel who sought to kill him. His wife Sepphora had the presence of mind to seize a knife and circumcise their eldest son, Gershom. "You are my bridegroom in blood and ours is a blood wedding," said she after saving his life.

We know the reason why Gershom had not been circumcised; Moses had promised his father-in-law, the priest Jethro, to bring up his first-born as a pagan. We are not told why God seems to have wanted Moses dead before he could accomplish his mission.

In Egypt Moses found conditions more than distressing: The Israelites were resigned to and wallowing in their suffering, which they had finally accepted. They could see no hope, envision no exciting prospect. When Moses and Aaron invited the elders of Israel to accompany them to Pharao's palace, the elders promised to follow them there. But as the elders came closer to their destination, there remained fewer and fewer. By the time Moses and Aaron arrived, the two brothers were alone.

The Talmud stresses this point by raising the question: One understands why Moses deserved his position of leader, since it was he who had negotiated the exodus with Pharao—but Aaron? How had he earned the title of high-priest? The answer is significant: While Moses was arguing with Pharao to grant the Israelites permission to leave, Aaron was arguing with the Israelites to agree to leave.

The meeting between the two brothers and Pharao was stormy—especially since Pharao had been in the midst of dictating his mail to seventy scribes writing his letters in seventy languages. At the sight of Moses and Aaron, the frightened scribes dropped their quills and papers and fell to their knees. Then, Moses and Aaron addressed their request to the king: "In the name of the God of Israel, we ask of you to let our people go." But Pharao became angry: "Who is this God you speak of? What is his name? And what does His power consist of? How many lands, how many provinces, how many cities has He conquered? How many wars has He won?"

Moses and Aaron tried to explain the inexplicable—that divine power has nothing to do with human ambition; it fills the universe and dominates its elements. "It is He who every day decides who shall live and who shall die...." Pharao then ordered all the chronicles of all the nations brought before him so that he might find in them the name of Israel's God. Recorded there were all the names of the gods of Moab, and the gods of Ammon and the gods of Zidion—but not the name of the one referred to by Moses and Aaron. Faced with this, Moses and Aaron offered him the explanation: "You are mad, Sire, you are seeking the living in the graves of the dead! All these names of all these idols in all these chronicles are dead, whereas our God is living...." But Pharao remained obstinate and replied: "Well, I don't know Him."

And so God decided to punish Pharao.

The plagues, which numbered ten, followed one another but did not resemble one another. Rivers of blood, nights of death. Nature turned against the inhabitants of the land. Time itself became hostile toward them. Plunged into total darkness, they no longer could see one another; everyone lived and suffered alone and could see nothing else. Then came the deaths of all the first-born, bringing mourning into every house, proving that justice can be blind, striking as it did the innocent, when it was meant for their parents. At last, Pharao, on his knees, submitted to the will of Israel's history.

The first two curses were provoked by Aaron and not by Moses. It was he and not his brother who struck the waters to bring forth the blood and the frogs. Why? Because Moses, saved by the waters, remained grateful to them.

Gratitude: A cardinal virtue of Moses. Of all the names he had been given, he retained the name Moses—the one given to him by Batya, the Pharao's daughter to whom he owed his life.

The exodus took place at night. Pharao insisted that the Israelites go as quickly as possible. Let them take along anything they wished, but let them go. Other slaves, as well, seized the opportunity and left for freedom before it was too late.

The very next day, Pharao had changed his mind. He gave orders to pursue the former slaves. Too late. On the seventh day, the Israelites crossed the Red Sea, leaving behind forever the Egyptians, many of whom drowned. This miracle inspired Moses—the stutterer—to compose his most beautiful, his most majestic song. It was so beautiful that even the angels above wanted to join into song with him, like him and the Israelites, but God silenced them: "My creatures are drowning," He said, "and you feel like singing?"

Whenever men die, God listens to the silence and weeps.

Meanwhile, the freed slaves were jubilant. Having seen their persecutors perish in the sea, they were shouting that now they could return to Egypt. They were hungry and thirsty in the desert. But Moses made them understand that their adventure had a higher goal, a more sacred meaning than their physical liberation.

Seven weeks later he made them gather at the foot of Mount Sinai and in the midst of a silence preceded by thunder and lightning, God revealed His Law to them.

And as heaven and earth shook, kings everywhere thought the end of the world had come. But their prophet Balaam reassured them: Nothing would be destroyed by fire or flood, it was only God presenting His Law to His people. Hearing this, the kings all cried out: "May He grant peace to His people," and felt a peace themselves.

But the Israelites refused to receive the Law; they were frightened by its demands. And so God lifted a mountain and, suspending it over their heads, told them: "If you accept my Law, you shall live; if you reject it, you shall perish on this very spot." In response, they all shouted: 'Yes, we accept it, yes, we accept You, yes, we shall obey You!"

And at that moment, one hundred and twenty myriads of angels came down from heaven and placed an invisible crown on the head of every participant, a crown which later was withdrawn when the people, in a moment of obliviousness and impatience, began to dance around the Golden Calf.

Had it not been for the episode of the Golden Calf, Israel would have remained a people of immortals. Now it is only an immortal people.

On that fateful day God decreed that as punishment they would forever study the Torah in sorrow, not only in joy, and in exile, not only in freedom.

How is one to explain this turnabout of the chosen people? How could they, only forty days after the revelation at Sinai, celebrate the divinity of an object?

The blame must be placed on Satan, says the Talmud.

As he was leaving them to start his ascension to heaven, Moses promised the Israelites to return at the end of forty days, bringing with him two tablets of the Law. But, at noontime of the last day, Satan succeded in showing them a false image of Moses stretched out on his death-bed, suspended between heaven and earth. And the people began to cry: "He is dead, our liberator has been killed...."And out of despair, they lost their heads and fashioned for themselves a Golden Calf which nobody could ever kill.

In his anger, Moses smashed the tablets of the Law. Yet, when he found himself face to face with God, he defended his people: "You kept them in Egypt, among the idol worshipers, for such a long time, how can you blame them now for their relapse?"

And God agreed to renew the experiment. Moses went back up to heaven and brought back the second tablets of the Law. This time the Jews received him without ceremony, in total silence. There is another difference: The first tablets were the work of God—the second were not; they were the work of man.

During the forty years of the desert crossing, Moses encountered many bitter disappointments. The never-ending complaints, the recriminations, the dissensions, the revolts, the pettiness he had to face day after day—how did he manage not to lose faith and courage? Perhaps therein lay his true greatness: He knew how not to despair.

People spoke ill of him, sought to quarrel with him. They reproached him for having married a pagan woman, they pushed him to the limits of his endurance. Sometimes he became angry, but still he always forgave.

As he came closer to his goal, he chose twelve notables and named them his scouts. Their mission? To penetrate into the land of Canaan and bring back a report. Of the twelve, ten returned disappointed and discouraged. They had found a wasteland, impoverished and in mourning—but with powerful, terribly powerful inhabitants.

Their conclusion: Not to go there—it would be better to go anywhere else but there. Some even went so far as to suggest a return to Egypt. And because almost a majority of the people chose to believe the pessimistic spies, the Israelites were doomed to stay yet another span of time in the desert. Thus only two of the scouts, Joshua and Caleb, who remained enthusiastic, succeeded in completing the entire journey from Egypt to Canaan: All of the other Israelites knew only one or the other.

Every year, on the anniversary of the scouts' return, Moses would order the Israelites to dig their own graves and spend the night in them. The next day, the heralds would call out the order: "Let the living separate themselves from the dead." And thus it was done. On the fortieth anniversary, all rose—for all of them already belonged to the new generation. They were worthy of entering The Promised Land, for slavery was no longer a temptation for them.

Then came the turn for Moses himself to leave this world. He knew it but opposed it. Wearing sackcloth and covered with ashes, he traced a circle around himself and implored God to let him live. Even if he was not to enter the Promised Land, even if he was to live far from honors, far from power. Even if he was to live like a beast or a bird. To convince him otherwise, God permitted him to live one day as disciple of his disciple and successor, Joshua. And when Moses felt jealousy distorting and dominating him, he cried out: "Rather a thousand deaths than a single moment of jealousy."

Nevertheless, he asked God not to let him die at the hands of the Angel of Death. Thus it was God himself who took the soul of Moses with a kiss.

Earlier Moses had blessed the tribes of Israel and told them of his last wish: To remember His Law and transmit it, and sing it from generation to generation as a message of life and beauty and a call for hope.

And God told Moses to climb the mountain. To isolate himself. To lie down. To stretch out his legs, his arms. To close his eyes. And listen.

Moses left this world, clinging to the voice of God.

Down below the people cried, as did all creation. And sometimes at night one can hear them still.

LIST OF
PAINTINGS

In the beginning God created the heaven and earth. Now the earth was unformed and void, and darkness was upon the face of the deep; and the spirit of God hovered over the face of the waters.

And God said: 'Let there be light.' And there was light. And God saw the light, that it was good; and God divided the light from the darkness.

And God called the light Day, and the darkness He called Night. And there was evening and there was morning, one day. Gen. 1:1-5.

THE CREATION OF
LIGHTS

9″ x 12″, 1964, tempera
on paper, collection of
Daniel Doron.

And God said: 'Let there be lights in the firmament of the heaven to divide the day from the night; and let them be for signs, and for seasons, and for days and years; and let them be for lights in the firmament of the heaven to give light upon the earth.' And it was so. And God made the two great lights: the greater light to rule the day, and the lesser light to rule the night; and the stars. And God set them in the firmament of the heaven to give light upon the earth, and to rule over the day and over the night, and to divide the light from the darkness; and God saw that it was good. And there was evening and there was morning, a fourth day.   Gen. 1:14-19.

82

THE BIRDS OF PARADISE

13″x 21″, 1965, acrylic on paper, collection of Daniel Doron.

שלום מושקוביץ הגלילי צפת הֹ נֹבֹ אֹתֹ

And God said: 'Let the waters swarm with swarms of living creatures, and let fowl fly above the earth in the open firmament of heaven.' And God created the great sea-monsters, and every living creature that creepeth, wherewith the waters swarmed, after its kind, and every winged fowl after its kind; and God saw that it was good. And God blessed them, saying: 'Be fruitful, and multiply, and fill the waters in the seas, and let fowl multiply in the earth.' And there was evening and there was morning, a fifth day. Gen. 1:20-23.

THE CREATION OF BEASTS
13″ x 19″, 1960, tempera on paper, collection of Daniel Doron.

And God said: 'Let the earth bring forth the living creature after its kind, cattle, and creeping thing, and beast of the earth after its kind.' And it was so. And God made the beast of the earth after its kind, and the cattle after their kind, and every thing that creepeth upon the ground after its kind; and God saw that it was good.

Gen. 1:24-25.

RECEIVING THE
SABBATH

20″ x 30″, 1969, acrylic
on paper, collection of
Daniel Doron.

*Shalom enclosed his
close-up views of people
celebrating the Sabbath
in the synagogue, and
the home within a pano-
ramic view of the city. He
encompassed the trees
within a view of orchards
growing on the hills
surrounding the city.*

A nd the heaven and the earth were finished, and all the host of them. And on the seventh day God finished His work which He had made; and He rested on the seventh day from all his work which He had made. And God blessed the seventh day, and hallowed it; because that in it He rested from all His work which God in creating had made.   Gen. 2:1-3.

THE EXPULSION FROM
EDEN

14" x 20", 1959, tempera
on paper, collection of
Daniel Doron.

*Because the Cherubim
brandished a sword
which "turned every
way," Shalom painted
an angel whose hands
and wings point both
ways. Later, the angel
arrives with his dog to
chase Adam and Eve
from Paradise. When
they lost their innocence,
Adam and Eve covered
their nakedness with fig
leaves. Eve wore a wig, to
modestly cover her hair;
however, living in a state
of nature before the
Torah was given, she did
not cover her breasts.*

And the Lord God said: 'Behold, the man is become as one of us, to know good and evil; and now, lest he put forth his hand, and take also of the tree of life, and eat, and live for ever.' Therefore the Lord God sent him forth from the garden of Eden, to till the ground from whence he was taken. So He drove out the man; and He placed at the east of the garden of Eden the cherubim, and the flaming sword which turned every way, to keep the way to the tree of life.

Gen. 3:22-24.

THE GIANTS AND THE
MEN OF RENOWN

13" x 20", 1970, acrylic
on paper, collection of
Daniel Doron.

*In the upper right-hand
corner are Adam and
Eve, and beneath them,
their descendants, sons
to the right, daughters to
the left. Lower, Shalom
depicts the further mul-
tiplication of people.
Further down, the wing-
ed sons of God are select-
ing their wives. Below
them, the giants and
men of renown. Finally,
a rearing lion and an en-
counter between a dog
and a snake intensify the
savage and violent
atmosphere of these wild
times.*

Αnd it came to pass, when men began to multiply on the face of the earth, and daughters were born unto them, that the sons of God saw the daughters of men that they were fair; and they took them wives, whomsoever they chose. And the Lord said: 'My spirit shall not abide in man for ever, for that he also is flesh: therefore shall his days be a hundred and twenty years.' The Nephilim were in the earth in those days, and also after that, when the sons of God came unto the daughters of men, and they bore children to them; the same were the mighty men that were of old, the men of renown.

Gen. 6:1-4.

NOAH, HIS FAMILY,
AND THE ANIMALS
ENTERING THE ARK

14" x 22", 1959, tempera
on paper, collection
of Dr. and Mrs. M.L.
Wiener.

*Noah, his sons and their
wives prepare for the
voyage in the ark. Noah
is picking figs, but his
wife is not seen. At the
bottom, the family pre-
pares to enter the ark.
Now all are present, in-
cluding Noah's wife.
Shem and his wife,
however, are set apart,
apparently in respect for
his separate destiny as
the progenitor of the
patriarchs.*

In the selfsame day entered Noah, and Shem, and Ham, and Japheth, the sons of Noah, and Noah's wife, and the three wives of his sons with them, into the ark; they, and every beast after its kind, and all the cattle after their kind, and every creeping thing that creepeth upon the earth after its kind, and every fowl after its kind, every bird of every sort. And they went in unto Noah into the ark, two and two of all flesh wherein is the breath of life. And they that went in, went in male and female of all flesh, as God commanded him; and the Lord shut him in.   Gen. 7:13-16.

THE DOVE RETURNS TO
NOAH'S ARK

20″ x 26″, 1963, tempera
on paper, collection of
Daniel Doron.

*The receding waters of
the flood reveal defoli-
ated trees, and corpses
floating in the water
with parted hair and
Hitlerian moustaches.
The water-soaked earth
is dark brown, but a
strip on top is already
green, anticipating new
vegetation and life. (In
a subsequent painting,
housed in the collec-
tion of The Museum of
Modern Art, New York,
the process is further ad-
vanced, with the drained
earth much lighter in
color and sprigs of new
vegetation budding.
Occasionally, Shalom
developed a sequence of
events in a series of
paintings, sometimes
done consecutively, and
sometimes months or
years apart.)*

And he stayed yet other seven days; and again he sent forth the dove out of the ark. And the dove came in to him at eventide; and lo in her mouth an olive-leaf freshly pluck-ed; so Noah knew that the waters were abated from off the earth. And he stayed yet other seven days; and sent forth the dove; and she returned not again unto him any more.

Gen. 8:10-12.

NOAH, HIS FAMILY,
AND THE ANIMALS
LEAVING THE ARK

18″ x 12″, 1958, tempera
on paper, collection of
Dr. and Mrs. Sam D.
Shrut.

And Noah went forth, and his sons, and his
wife, and his sons' wives with him; every
beast, every creeping thing, and every fowl,
whatsoever moveth upon the earth, after their
families, went forth out of the ark.   Gen. 8:18-19.

וירד ה' לראת את העיר ואת המגדל אשר בנו בני האדם   ויפץ ה' אתם משם על פני כל הארץ ויחדלו לבנת העיר   (שלום מושקוביץ הגלילי צפת
אנשי בבל בונים את המגדל והמלאך והמלאך יורד מן השמים להפיצם בארץ

מגדל בבל

THE TOWER OF BABEL
TOPPLED

14″ x 10″, 1963, tempera
on paper, collection of
Daniel Doron.

*The top of the tower
reaches to heaven, and
is swallowed by clouds.
The angel brandishes
his sword, scattering
those who would chal-
lenge God.*

So the Lord scattered them abroad from
thence upon the face of all the earth; and
they left off to build the city. Therefore was the
name of it called Babel; because the Lord did
there confound the language of all the earth;
and from thence did the Lord scatter them
abroad upon the face of all the earth. Gen. 11:8-9.

THE TOWER OF BABEL
14" x 20", 1963, tempera
on paper, collection of
Daniel Doron.

And the whole earth was of one language and of one speech. And it came to pass, as they journeyed east, that they found a plain in the land of Shinar; and they dwelt there. And they said one to another:'Come, let us make brick, and burn them thoroughly.' And they had brick for stone, and slime had they for mortar. And they said: 'Come, let us build us a city, and a tower, with its top in heaven, and let us make us a name; lest we be scattered abroad upon the face of the whole earth.' And the Lord came down to see the city and the tower, which the children of men builded.   Gen. 11:1-5.

ABRAHAM AND LOT
LEAVE FOR
THE PROMISED LAND

20" x 14", 1960, tempera
on paper, collection of
Daniel Doron.

Now the Lord said unto Abram: 'Get thee out of thy country, and from thy kindred, and from thy father's house, unto the land that I will show thee. And I will make of thee a great nation, and I will bless thee, and make thy name great; and be thou a blessing. And I will bless them that bless thee, and him that curseth thee will I curse; and in thee shall all the families of the earth be blessed.' So Abram went, as the Lord had spoken unto him; and Lot went with him; and Abram was seventy and five years old when he departed out of Haran. And Abram took Sarai his wife, and Lot his brother's son, and all their substance that they had gathered, and the souls that they had gotten in Haran; and they went forth to go into the land of Canaan; and into the land of Canaan they came.

Gen. 12:1-5.

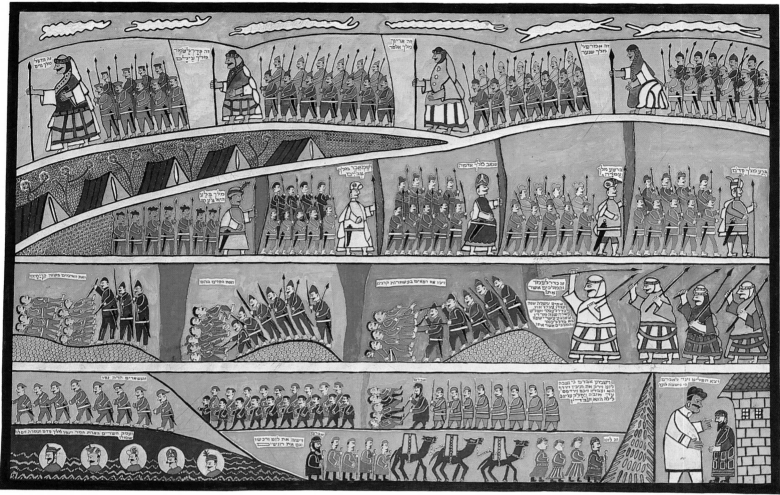

ABRAHAM AND THE
NINE KINGS

29" x 19", 1964,
tempera on paper,
collection of Israel
Museum, Jerusalem.

*An example of Shalom's
artful use of the contin-
uous pictorial narrative.
In the top tier are the
four kings and their
armies, who later defeat
the five kings arrayed in
the second tier, in a battle joined in the third
tier. In the bottom tier,*

*on the right, a refugee
from the battle informs
Abraham that Lot and
his family have been
taken prisoners. In the
top half of the bottom
tier, Abraham's men
rescue Lot from the
victorious armies. In the
lower half, Lot and his
family return. On the
left, soldiers flee after the
battles on the top. Below
them the five kings are
trapped in lime pits. Distinct headgear identifies
each of them.*

And there went out the king of Sodom, and the king of Gomorrah, and the king of Admah, and the king of Zeboiim, and the king of Bela—the same is Zoar; and they set the battle in array against them in the vale of Siddim; against Chedorlaomer king of Elam, and Tidal king of Goiim, and Amraphel king of Shinar, and Arioch king of Ellasar; four kings against the five. Now the vale of Siddim was full of slime pits; and the kings of Sodom and Gomorrah fled, and they fell there, and they that remained fled to the mountain. And they took all the goods of Sodom and Gomorrah, and all their victuals, and went their way. And they took Lot, Abram's brother's son, who dwelt in Sodom, and his goods, and departed.

And there came one that had escaped, and told Abram the Hebrew—now he dwelt by the terebinths of Mamre the Amorite, brother of Eschol, and brother of Aner; and these were confederate with Abram. And when Abram heard that his brother was taken captive, he led forth his trained men, born in his house, three hundred and eighteen, and pursued as far as Dan. And he divided himself against them by night, he and his servants, and smote them, and pursued them unto Hobah, which is on the left hand of Damascus. And he brought back all the goods, and also brought back his brother Lot, and his goods, and the women also, and the people. Gen. 14:8-16.

GOD'S COVENANT WITH
ABRAHAM

14" x 19", 1965, acrylic
on paper, collection of
Daniel Doron.

*The land of Canaan,
which Abraham's chil-
dren will inherit, is at
the top. Abraham, on the
right, counts the stars,
and a hand shaped like a
"yad" points at them.
Shalom uses the hand
with a pointing forefin-
ger, corresponding to the
"yad," a pointer used to
read the Torah in syna-
gogue, to focus on an im-
portant section, event, or
person in his paintings.
The bird of prey swoops
down on the sacrifice.
Below, in his sleep,
Abraham has a vision
of God appearing from
within the blood-red
cloud.*

And He said unto him: 'I am the Lord that brought thee out of Ur of the Chaldees, to give thee this land to inherit it.' And he said: 'O Lord God, whereby shall I know that I shall inherit it?' And He said unto him: 'Take Me a heifer of three years old, and a she-goat of three years old, and a ram of three years old, and a turtle-dove, and a young pigeon.' And he took him all these, and divided them in the midst, and laid each half over against the other; but the birds divided he not. And the birds divided he not. And the birds of prey came down upon the carcasses, and Abram drove them away. And it came to pass, that, when the sun was going down, a deep sleep fell upon Abram; and, lo, a dread, even a great darkness, fell upon him. And He said unto Abram: 'Know of a surety that thy seed shall be a stranger in a land that is not theirs, and shall serve them; and they shall afflict them four hundred years; and also that nation, whom they shall serve, will I judge; and afterward shall they come out with great substance. But thou shalt go to thy fathers in peace; thou shalt be buried in a good old age. And in the fourth generation they shall come back hither; for the iniquity of the Amorite is not yet full.' And it came to pass, that, when the sun went down, and there was thick darkness, behold a smoking furnace, and a flaming torch that passed between these pieces. Gen. 15:7-17.

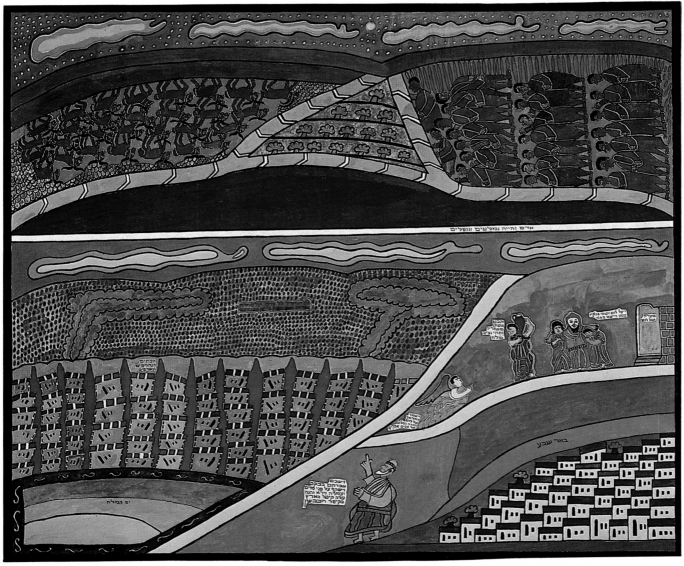

THE RUIN OF SODOM
AND GOMORRAH

28" x 23", 1964, tempera
on paper, collection of
Daniel Doron.

*The dead lie on their
backs, visually organ-
ized at the top to convey
the sense of upheaval
during the ruin of Sodom
and Gomorrah. Below,
a rain of fire and brim-
stone falls as smoke
rises in mushroom
clouds from toppling
houses that are on fire.
Bottom right, Abraham,
coming from the town
of Beersheba, watches
the cataclysm, pointing
at the fire and smoke.
Above him, the angel
directs Lot to the moun-
tain so he can escape.
Lot's wife turns around
and is transformed in-
to a pillar of salt. Lot
embraces his daughters
in front of his cave.*

Then the Lord caused to rain upon Sodom and upon Gomorrah brimstone and fire from the Lord out of heaven; and He overthrew those cities, and all the Plain, and all the inhabitants of the cities, and that which grew upon the ground. But his wife looked back from behind him, and she became a pillar of salt. And Abraham got up early in the morning to the place where he had stood before the Lord. And he looked out toward Sodom and Gomorrah, and toward all the land of the Plain, and beheld, and, lo, the smoke of the land went up as the smoke of a furnace.

Gen. 19:24-28.

ABRAHAM SETTLES IN
BEERSHEBA

19″ x 13″, 1957, gouache
on paper, collection
of Israel Museum,
Jerusalem.

*Abraham welcomes
visitors who pass the
tamarisk tree which he
planted. The writing
above Abraham reads,
"Shalom Aleichem!"—
Welcome in peace. The
structure at the center is
marked "Abraham's
house." In the back yard,
Ishmael, wearing a fez
and holding a large key,
approaches the house
with his retinue.*

And Abraham planted a tamarisk-tree in
Beer-sheba, and called there on the name
of the Lord, the Everlasting God.   Gen. 21:33.

ISAAC MEETING
REBECCA

14″ x 10″, 1966, tempera
on paper, collection of
Daniel Doron.

*The caravan led by Eliez-
er, Abraham's caretaker,
comes over the mountain,
and descends toward
the field where Isaac
"went out to meditate."*

And Isaac went out to meditate in the field at the eventide; and he lifted up his eyes, and saw, and, behold, there were camels coming. And Rebekah lifted up her eyes, and when she saw Isaac, she alighted from the camel. And she said unto the servant: 'What man is this that walketh in the field to meet us?' And the servant said: 'It is my master.' And she took her veil, and covered herself. And the servant told Isaac all the things that he had done.

Gen. 24:63-66.

98

יצחק   רבקה   אברהם   אליעזר עבד אברהם

ויקח יצחק את רבקה ויבאה האהלה שרה אמו ותהי־לו לאשה ויאהם יצחק אחרי אמו
מכת הכליגרף של יצחק ורבקה

(שלום משקובסקי הגלילי)

THE WEDDING OF
ISAAC AND REBECCA

14″ x 10″, 1966, tempera
on paper, collection of
Daniel Doron.

*The Bible tells us that
Isaac brought Rebecca
into his mother Sarah's
tent. Shalom apparently
could not conceive of the
patriarch's son leading
his wife into such tem-
porary quarters; instead
he painted a stone house,
with steps leading to a
front door, topped by a
carved tympanum. The
bridegroom carries an
enormous key. Abraham
and his caretaker, Eliez-
er, carry staffs crowned
with globes.*

And Isaac brought her into his mother
Sarah's tent, and took Rebekah, and she
became his wife; and he loved her. And Isaac
was comforted for his mother.   Gen. 24:67.

JACOB'S DREAM

13" x 19", 1967, acrylic on paper, collection of Daniel Doron.

The twelve angels on the ladder, and the twelve blossoms on the tree, represent the twelve tribes which Jacob will sire. On one side the count is only eleven; perhaps because the tribe of Levy was not given land. In his dream, Jacob envisions a figure in red, representing God.

And Jacob went out from Beersheba, and went toward Haran. And he lighted upon the place, and tarried there all night, because the sun was set; and he took one of the stones of the place, and put it under his head, and lay down in that place to sleep. And he dreamed, and behold a ladder set up on the earth, and the top of it reached to heaven; and behold the angels of God ascending and descending on it.

And, behold, the Lord stood beside him, and said: 'I am the Lord, the God of Abraham thy father, and the God of Isaac. The land whereon thou liest, to thee will I give it, and to thy seed. And thy seed shall be as the dust of the earth, and thou shalt spread abroad to the west, and to the east, and to the north, and to the south. And in thee and in thy seed shall all the families of the earth be blessed.   Gen.28:10-14.

JACOB WRESTLING
WITH THE ANGEL

12″ x 18″, 1963, tempera
on paper, collection of
D.M. Freidenberg.

ויותר יעקב לבדו ויאבק איש עמו עד עלות השחר   (בראשית לב, כה)

And Jacob was left alone; and there wrestled a man with him until the breaking of the day. And when he saw that he prevailed not against him, he touched the hollow of his thigh; and the hollow of Jacob's thigh was strained, as he wrestled with him. And he said: 'Let me go, for the day breaketh.' And he said: 'I will not let thee go, except thou bless me.' And he said unto him: 'What is thy name?' And he said: 'Jacob.' And he said: 'Thy name shall be called no more Jacob, but Israel; for thou hast striven with God and with men, and hast prevailed.' And Jacob asked him, and said: 'Tell me, I pray thee, thy name.' And he said: 'Wherefore is it that thou dost ask after my name?' And he blessed him there. And Jacob called the name of the place Peniel: 'for I have seen God face to face, and my life is preserved.' And the sun rose upon him as he passed over Peniel, and he limped upon his thigh.

Gen. 32:25-32.

MOSES FOUND IN THE
BULRUSHES

8″ x 10½″, 1965, tempera
on paper, collection of
Daniel Doron.

*Pharoah's daughter,
under the parasol,
points at Moses and one
of her maids reaches out
to him. Miriam watches
the scene.*

And there went a man of the house of Levi, and took to wife a daughter of Levi. And the woman conceived, and bore a son; and when she saw him that he was a goodly child, she hid him three months. And when she could not longer hide him, she took for him an ark of bulrushes, and daubed it with slime and with pitch; and she put the child therein, and laid it in the flags by the river's brink. And his sister stood afar off, to know what would be done to him. And the daughter of Pharoah came down to bathe in the river; and her maidens walked along by the river-side; and she saw the ark among the flags, and sent her handmaid to fetch it. And she opened it, and saw it, even the child; and behold a boy that wept. And she had compassion on him, and said: 'This is one of the Hebrews' children.' Then said his sister to Pharoah's daughter: 'Shall I go and call thee a nurse of the Hebrew women, that she may nurse the child for thee?'

Exod. 2:1-7.

MOSES AND THE BURN-
ING BUSH

20″ x 14″, 1962, tempera
on paper, collection of
Daniel Doron.

*Shalom divides his
painting into secular
(light area on the right)
and holy ground (in-
tense area to the left).
Moses' discarded
shoes—like Jacob's
sandals—are placed in
secular ground within
the holy area.*

Now Moses was keeping the flock of Jethro his father-in-law, the priest of Midian; and he led the flock to the farthest end of the wilderness, and came to the mountain of God, unto Horeb. And the angel of the Lord appeared unto him in a flame of fire out of the midst of a bush; and he looked, and, behold, the bush burned with fire, and the bush was not consumed. And Moses said: 'I will turn aside now, and see this great sight, why the bush is not burnt.' And when the Lord saw that he turned aside to see, God called unto him out of the midst of the bush, and said: 'Moses, Moses.' And he said: 'Here am I.' And He said: 'Draw not nigh hither; put off thy shoes from off thy feet, for the place whereon thou standest is holy ground.   Exod. 3:1-5.

MOSES ANNOUNCING
THE HOLIDAYS
14" x 11", 1967, acrylic
on paper, collection of
Daniel Doron.

And the Lord spoke unto Moses, saying: Speak unto the children of Israel, and say unto them: The appointed seasons of the Lord, which ye shall proclaim to be holy convocations, even these are My appointed seasons.

Lev. 23:1-2.

And the Lord said unto Moses: 'Say unto Aaron: Take thy rod, and stretch out thy hand over the waters of Egypt, over their rivers, over their streams, and over their pools, and over all their ponds of water, that they may become blood; and there shall be blood throughout all the land of Egypt, both in vessels of wood and in vessels of stone.'

Exod. 7:19.

And Aaron stretched out his hand over the waters of Egypt; and the frogs came up, and covered the land of Egypt.

Exod. 8:2.

...and Aaron stretched out his hand with his rod, and smote the dust of the earth, and there were gnats upon men, and upon beast...

Exod. 8:13.

THE TEN PLAGUES

18″ x 24″, 1965, tempera
on paper, collection of
Daniel Doron.

...and there came grievous swarms of flies into the house of the pharoah, and into his servants' houses; and in all the land of Egypt...

Exod. 8:20.

Behold, the hand of the Lord is upon thy cattle which are in the field, upon the horses, upon the asses, upon the camels, upon the herds, and upon the flock; there shall be a very grievous murrain.

Exodus. 9:3.

And the Lord said unto Moses and unto Aaron: 'Take to you handfuls of soot of the furnace, and let Moses throw it heavenward in the sight of the Pharoah. And it shall become small dust over all the land of Egypt, and shall be a boil breaking forth with blains upon man and upon beast, throughout all the land of Egypt.'

Exod. 9:8-9.

And Moses stretched forth his rod towards heaven; and the Lord sent thunder and hail...

Exod. 9:23.

And the locusts went up over all the land of Egypt...

Exod. 10:14.

And Moses stretched forth his hand toward heaven; and there was a thick darkness in all the land of Egypt three days...

Exod. 10:22.

And Moses said: 'Thus saith the Lord: About midnight will I go out into the midst of Egypt; and all the first-born in the land of Egypt shall die, from the first-born of Pharaoh that sitteth upon his throne, even unto the first-born of the maid-servant that is behind the mill; and all the first-born of cattle.'

Exod. 11:4.

THE NIGHT OF
REDEMPTION

18″ x 24″, 1965, tempera
on paper, collection of
Daniel Doron.

*The black angel, the dark-
ened portals, the empty
chair, and the ink-blue
sky represent death. The
green trees, the green
portals, the flowering
branch, and the abstract
depiction of the Holy
Land represent redemp-
tion.*

And it came to pass at midnight, that the Lord smote all the first-born in the land of Egypt, from the first-born of Pharaoh that sat on his throne unto the first-born of the captive that was in the dungeon; and all the first-born of cattle. And Pharaoh rose up in the night, he, and all his servants, and all the Egyptians; and there was a great cry in Egypt; for there was not a house where there was not one dead.

Exod. 12:29-30.

106

THE EXODUS WITH THE
PILLAR OF FIRE

37″ x 21″, 1967, acrylic
on canvas, collection of
Daniel Doron.

*During the night, the
Israelites are led by a pillar of fire and smoke.
Reading from bottom left,
the caravan wends its
way upward towards the
Promised Land. The
major thrust of the com-
position is in the upper
panel, moving in the di-
rection of Hebrew script.
Moses leads the proces-
sion with a staff in his
hands.*

And it came to pass the selfsame day that the Lord did bring the children of Israel out of the land of Egypt by their hosts.   Exod. 12:51.

And the Lord went before them by day in a pillar of cloud, to lead them the way; and by night in a pillar of fire, to give them light; that they might go by day and by night.   Exod. 13:21.

MOSES ON SINAI
AND THE FEAST OF
SHAVU'OT

20½" x 29½", 1969, acrylic on paper, collection of Daniel Doron.

"The top half of the picture shows the giving of the law, and the bottom half shows how the Jews in the synagogue, at home and in the streets are celebrating the feast of Shavu'ot." These are Shalom's own words written, in Yiddish, at the bottom. In the upper half, rows of people, approaching the mountain from the tent camp, are seen from behind; they are not blindfolded as many assume. In the grey tier, people move about in agitation; above them, lightning and the ram's horn—or Shofar—can be seen.

In the bottom half, Shalom frames his close-ups within a panoramic view. On the horizon are diminutive shapes of houses and trees; closer by, the town on the hillside and the olive groves that surround it. In between are three people "doing their shopping for the holiday," Shalom wrote. Underneath, in a horizontal band, are greens that are also seen festooned inside the synagogue and the home, a traditional decoration for this holiday.

And it came to pass on the third day, when it was morning, that there were thunders and lightnings and a thick cloud upon the mount, and the voice of a horn exceedingly loud; and all the people that were in the camp trembled. And Moses brought forth the people out of the camp to meet God; and they stood at the nether part of the mount. Exod. 19:16-17.

108

MOSES RECEIVING THE
LAW

18½" x 13", 1957,
tempera on paper,
collection of Israel
Museum, Jerusalem.

And the Lord spoke unto Moses: 'Go, get thee down; for thy people that thou broughtest up out of the land of Egypt, have dealt corruptly; they have turned aside quickly out of the way which I commanded them; they have made them a molten calf and have worshipped it, and have sacrificed unto it, and said: This is thy god, O Israel, which brought thee up out of the land of Egypt.'

Exod. 32:7-8.

THE EXODUS WITH THE
PILLAR OF SMOKE

27″ x 19″, 1966, acrylic
on paper, collection of
Daniel Doron.

And it came to pass the selfsame day that the Lord did bring the children of Israel out of the land of Egypt by their hosts.　Exod. 12:51.

And the Lord went before them by day in a pillar of cloud, to lead them the way; and by night in a pillar of fire, to give them light; that they might go by day and by night.　Exod. 13:21.

MOSES BREAKING THE
TABLETS OF THE LAW

19″ x 13″, 1963, tempera
on paper, collection of
Daniel Doron.

And Moses turned, and went down from the mount, with the two tables of the testimony in his hands...And it came to pass, as soon as he came nigh unto the camp, that he saw the calf and the dancing; and Moses' anger waxed hot, and he cast the tables out of his hands, and broke them beneath the mount.

Exod. 32:15-19.

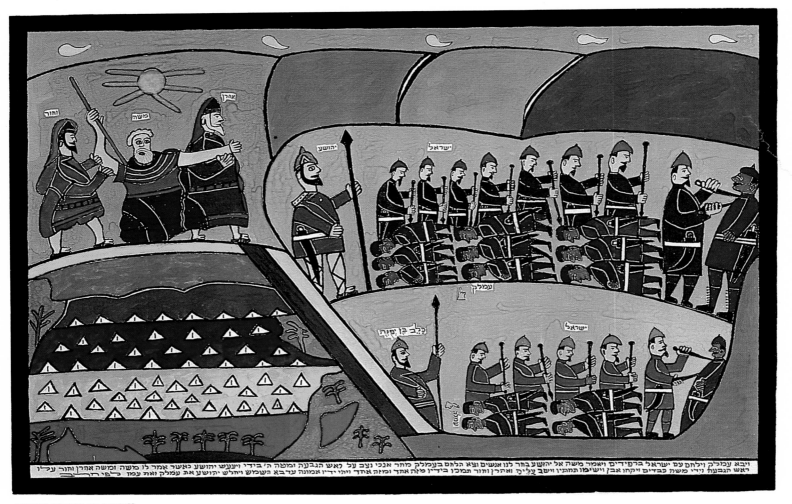

MOSES AT THE WAR WITH
AMALEK

17″ x 11″, 1964, tempera
on paper, collection of
Daniel Doron.

*Note the abstract panel
of fertile land at bottom
left containing the
Israelite's camp with
date palms during the
war with Amalek.*

So Joshua did as Moses had said to him, and fought with Amalek; and Moses, Aaron, and Hur went up to the top of the hill. And it came to pass, when Moses held up his hands, that Israel prevailed; and when he let down his hands, Amalek prevailed. But Moses' hands were heavy; and they took a stone, and put it under him, and he sat thereon; and Aaron and Hur stayed up his hands, the one on the one side, and the other on the other side; and his hands were steady until the going down of the sun.

Exod. 17:10-12.